The Genius Prince's Guide to Raising a Nation Out of Debt
(Hey, How About Treason?)

Toru Toba | Illustration **Falmaro**

"......"

With a dyed head of hair, Ninym flashed Wein a mischievous grin, pressing him for his opinion.

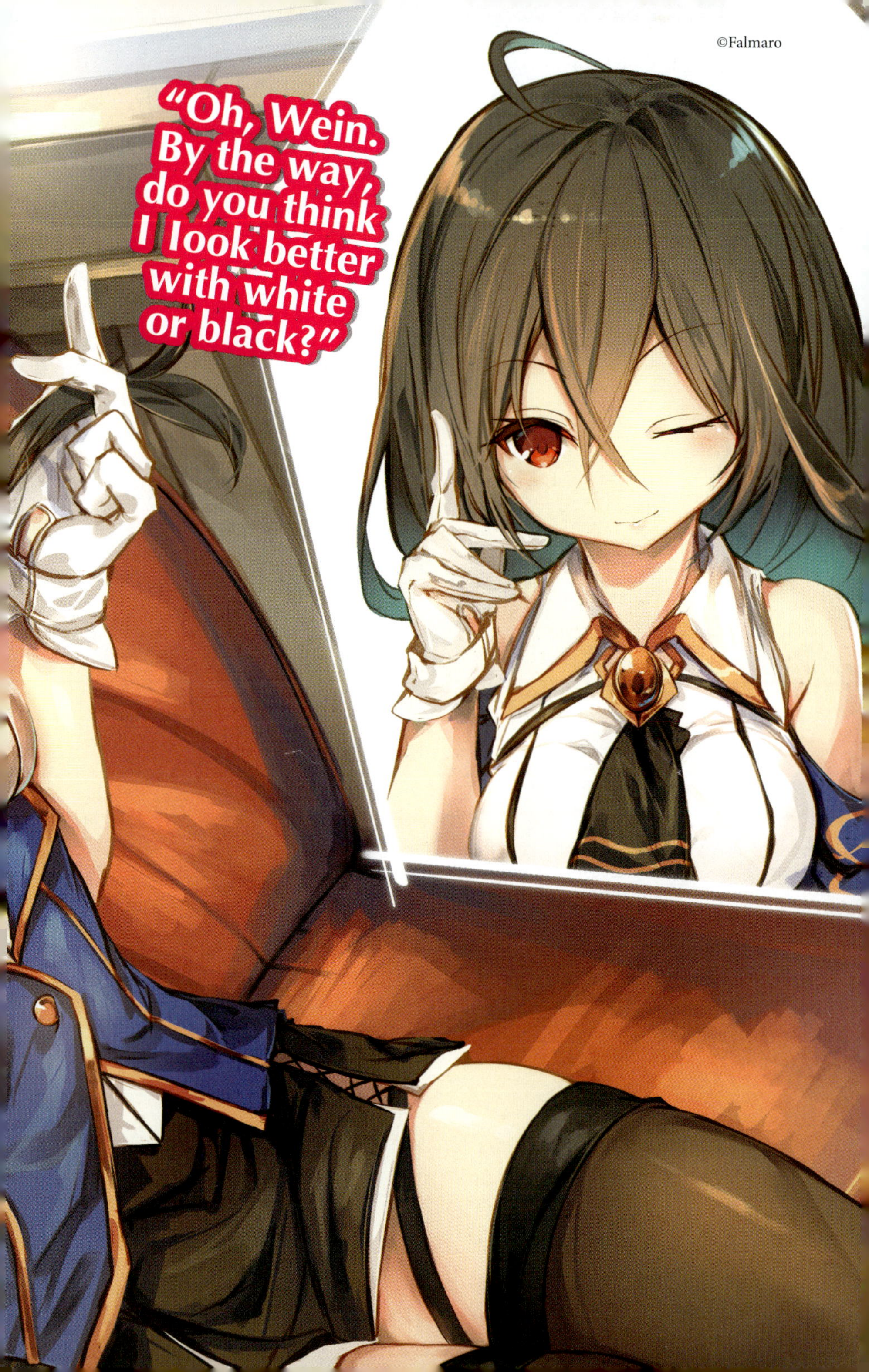
©Falmaro
"Oh, Wein. By the way, do you think I look better with white or black?"

"What could it be today?" Wein asked in response to Zeno's inquiry.

This had become their daily ritual as they made their way to the royal capital of Cavarin.

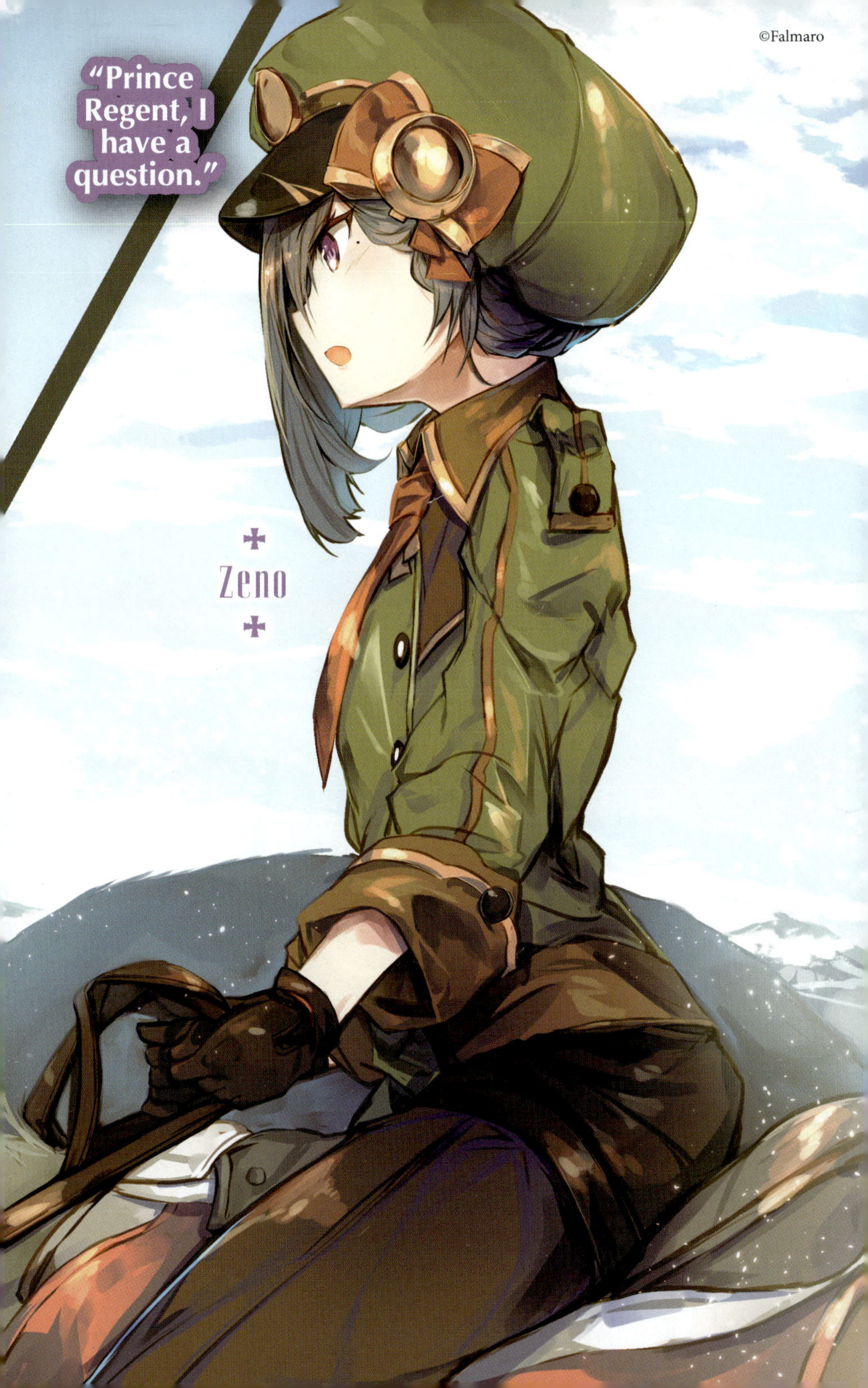
©Falmaro
"Prince Regent, I have a question."
Zeno

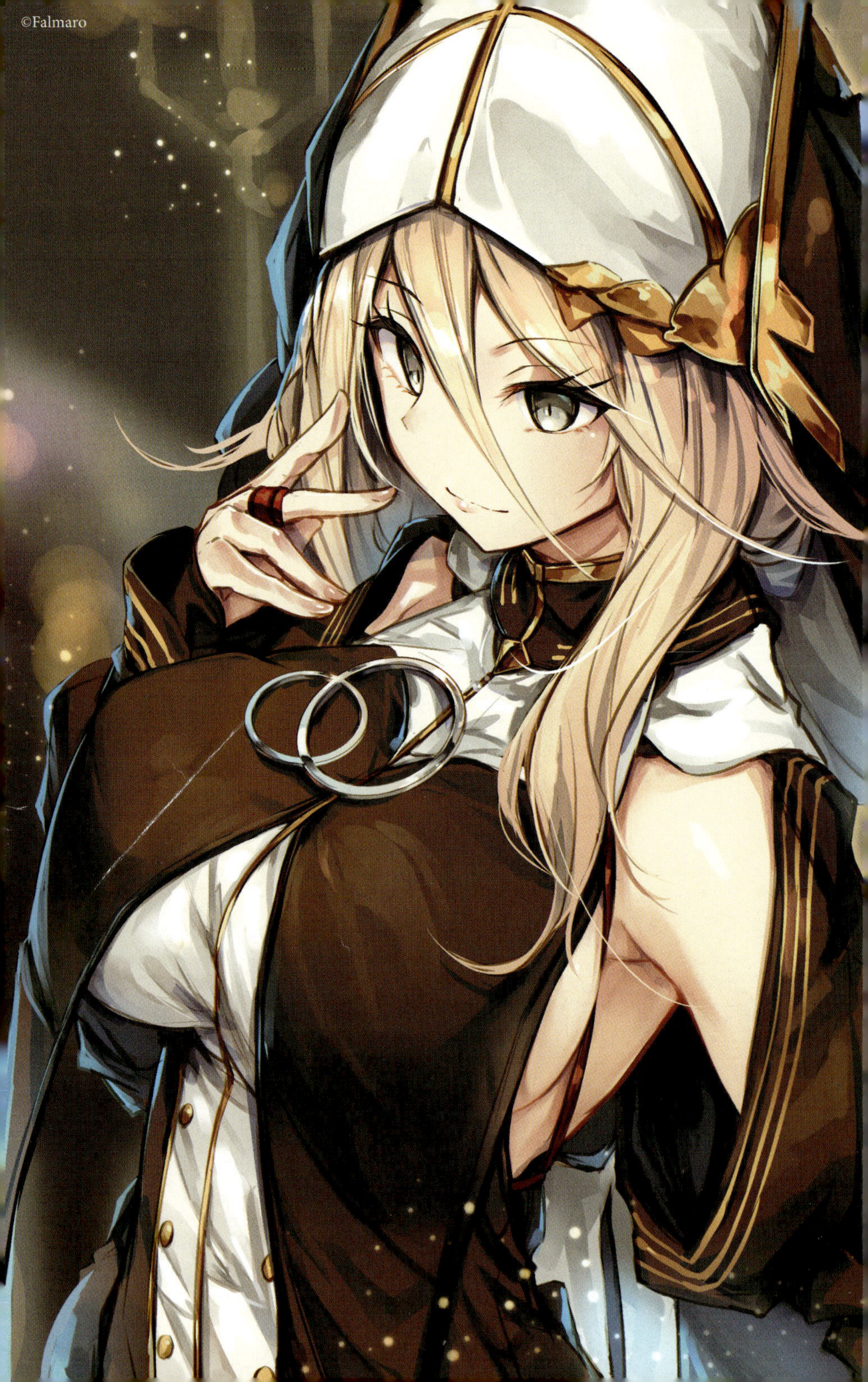
©Falmaro

Director of Levetia's Gospel Bureau

Caldmellia

"THANK YOU FOR COMING, CROWN PRINCE."

As the Holy King's assistant, the head of the Gospel Bureau had authority that rivaled the Holy Elites. Wein stared, fixated, at the dark horse who rose to political power in spite of the deep-seated misogyny of the West.

CONTENTS

The Genius Prince's Guide to Raising a Nation
Out of Debt (Hey, How About Treason?)

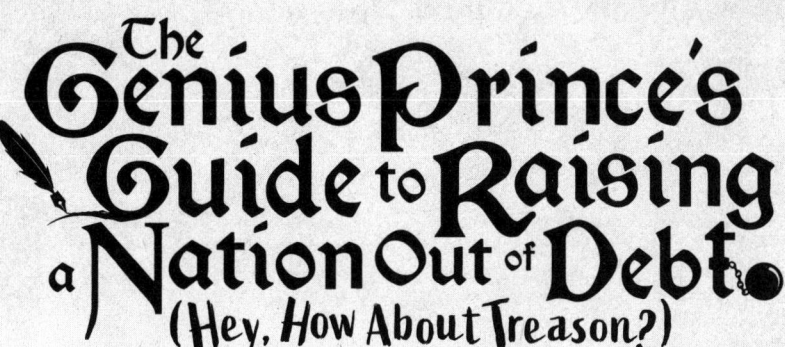

The Genius Prince's Guide to Raising a Nation Out of Debt
(Hey, How About Treason?)

3

Toru Toba
Illustration **Falmaro**

YEN ON

New York

The Genius Prince's Guide to Raising a Nation Out of Debt (Hey, How About Treason?)

3

Toru Toba

Translation by Jessica Lange
Cover art by Falmaro

This book is a work of fiction. Names, characters, places, and incidents are the product of the author's imagination or are used fictitiously. Any resemblance to actual events, locales, or persons, living or dead, is coincidental.

TENSAI OUJI NO AKAJI KOKKA SAISEI-JYUTSU ~ SOUDA, BAIKOKU SHIYOU ~ volume 3
Copyright © 2019 Toru Toba
Illustrations copyright © 2019 Falmaro
All rights reserved.
Original Japanese edition published in 2019 by SB Creative Corp.

This English edition is published by arrangement with SB Creative Corp., Tokyo, in care of Tuttle-Mori Agency, Inc., Tokyo.

English translation © 2020 by Yen Press, LLC

Yen On
150 West 30th Street, 19th Floor
New York, NY 10001

Visit us at yenpress.com
facebook.com/yenpress
twitter.com/yenpress
yenpress.tumblr.com
instagram.com/yenpress

First Yen On Edition: June 2020

Yen On is an imprint of Yen Press, LLC.
The Yen On name and logo are trademarks of Yen Press, LLC.

The publisher is not responsible for websites (or their content) that are not owned by the publisher.

Library of Congress Cataloging-in-Publication Data
Names: Toba, Toru, author. | Falmaro, illustrator. | Lange, Jessica (Translator), translator.
Title: The genius prince's guide to raising a nation out of debt (hey, how about treason?) / Toru Toba ; illustration by Falmaro ; translation by Jessica Lange.
Other titles: Tensai ouji no akaji kokka saisei-jyutsu, souda, baikoku shiyou. English
Description: First Yen On edition. | New York, NY: Yen On, 2019-
Identifiers: LCCN 2019017156 | ISBN 9781975385194 (v. 1 : pbk.) | ISBN 9781975385170 (v. 2 : pbk.) | ISBN 9781975309985 (v. 3 : pbk.)
Subjects: LCSH: Princes—Fiction.
Classification: LCC PL876.O25 T4613 2019 | DDC 895.6/36—dc23
LC record available at https://lccn.loc.gov/2019017156

ISBNs: 978-1-9753-0998-5 (paperback)
978-1-9753-0999-2 (ebook)

10 9 8 7 6 5 4 3 2 1

LSC-C

Printed in the United States of America

The Genius Prince's Guide to Raising a Nation Out of Debt
(Hey, How About Treason?)

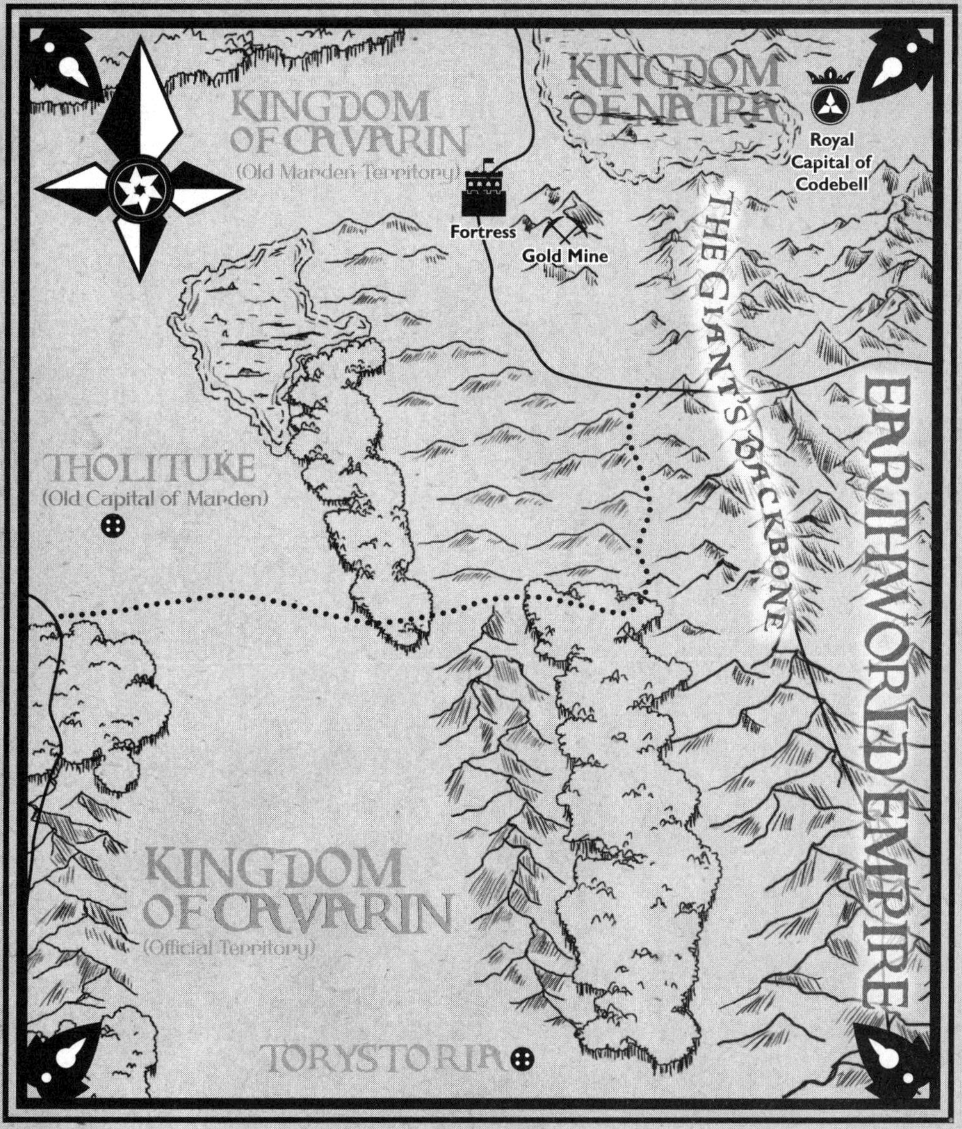
KINGDOM OF CAVARIN
(Old Marden Territory)
KINGDOM OF NATRA
Royal Capital of Codebell
Fortress
Gold Mine
THE GIANT'S BACKBONE
EARTHWORLD EMPIRE
THOLITUKE
(Old Capital of Marden)
KINGDOM OF CAVARIN
(Official Territory)
TORYSTORIA

For a while, it had gone unnoticed that no one had seen clouds heavy with snow in quite some time.

In its place, weak rays of light started to filter to the ground, gently settling onto the earth. Between piles of snow, green buds began pushing through the earth, and the wind had started to grow warm.

Soon, the animals that had managed to endure the cold would begin to stir.

Winter in Natra was coming to an end.

"Yawn…"

The warm sun poured through the windows, causing the crown princess of Natra, Falanya Elk Arbalest, to yawn just a little. She hurriedly clasped her hand over her mouth.

Casting a timid glance at the elderly man in front of her, she prayed he hadn't noticed.

However, this was Claudius, her instructor who had spent many years teaching noble children. There was no way her little wish would come true.

"It appears you are bored by my lesson."

"N-not at all, Claudius," Falanya replied, insisting on keeping up appearances. "I was hanging on every word. That was, um, because I had insufficient rest last night. I'm sure you know what's happening today."

"Hmm…" He considered her cheeky rebuttal. "In that case," he started again, with elderly mischief, "am I right to assume you know where we left off, Your Highness?"

"Of—of course!" Falanya yelped, her eyes scanning the textbook in her hands as she racked her mind for the last bits of Claudius's lecture. It had to be…around here…!

"It was about Naliavene, the homeland of Natra's founder, King Salema!"

"……" Claudius's eyes bored into her, as if to tell her to spit out what she was hiding, but she confidently met his eyes.

Her heart was pounding in her chest as she waited for him to say something.

All of a sudden, Claudius smiled. "I see. You were listening this whole time. An error on my part. Please forgive me, Princess Falanya."

"…It's all right, Claudius. Everyone makes mistakes." Falanya flashed a big smile even though on the inside she was breathing a mental sigh of relief. In her own estimation, the princess thought she looked all business. To everyone else, she still mostly came off as a small, adorable animal attempting to appear more intimidating by standing taller.

Claudius was proud of her progress. With feigned nonchalance, he thumbed through his textbook—to the section on Naliavene that Falanya had just referenced. If this was what she'd heard, so be it.

"Well, let us continue… Two hundred years ago, the western Kingdom of Naliavene had two princes, Galea and Salema. They were gifted and like-minded, known to the people as the Twin Swords of Vene."

One of the Twin Swords, Salema, had become the founding king of Natra. In other words, he was Falanya's ancestor.

"However, the princes were *too* talented, which created a particular issue. Princess Falanya, would you like to take a guess what the problem might have been?"

"Umm…" It could have been a number of things. She chose the one that seemed the most plausible. "Because it made it hard to choose the next heir?"

Claudius nodded. "Indeed. With each new accomplishment, the factions that sprung up around the two grew more powerful until not even the princes could control them anymore. They had always had a good relationship, and this unwanted antagonism caused them quite the headache."

"Wait a second. Didn't these princes have a father… The king? Couldn't he decide his successor?"

"The general consensus was that even the king could not control the factions… But according to the notes later left by King Salema, the princes' power frightened the ruler of Naliavene, which led him to intentionally pitting them against each other to protect his throne."

Falanya looked perplexed. "'To protect his throne'…? But wouldn't he have had to pass it on to one of the princes at some point?"

"Yes, that was unavoidable, but it's human nature for those with great power to delay losing it. This apprehension must have made him forget his duty as a parent and a king."

A grimace appeared on the princess's face. In Falanya's world, the royal family consisted of her, her older brother, and her father. As people, aristocrats, and family, her brother and father had set wonderful examples for her. It was hard to stomach the thought that a father—and king—would encourage his own children to fight among themselves.

"Whatever the truth of the situation, the internal conflict continued to intensify as the king failed to intervene. Nearby nations used this opportunity to invade Naliavene. But this was not enough to curb the factions and their one-track minds. Salema made an important decision under the belief that the nation was headed for destruction."

"I got it. He left the country, right?"

Falanya guessed Salema had come upon their shores and established Natra, but Claudius shook his head.

"No. He would have risked getting caught by his faction and been dragged back, forced to serve as their figurehead again. Even if he had managed to get away successfully, the remaining son and the king would have become locked in a power struggle, leaving them vulnerable to attacks of enemy nations. Salema desired internal unification of power…as soon as possible."

"So what did he do?"

Claudius was silent for a few moments before starting again in a level tone.

"They say it was in the audience hall. As the king sat on his throne, Salema approached, telling him he had an important matter to discuss. Then—he killed the king with a concealed knife."

Falanya's eyes widened. "He…*killed* him?! He killed the king…?! His own *father*?!"

"Yes. Other nations have recorded the event in the same way. There is no doubt." With Falanya—aghast—in his periphery, Claudius continued. "Salema was swiftly apprehended. It is said he did not resist. Assassinating the king is a heinous crime, and his faction fell apart. This helped Galea consolidate all power. He suppressed the chaos breaking out among the nobility and put a complete halt to foreign invasions."

"He…killed the king to protect the nation…"

She tried to picture it, placing herself in his shoes. Could she have done the same? She thought of the current king, her father, the one who she loved and admired. Imagined plunging a knife through him.

...*Absolutely not.* There was no way she could ever do it. It was impossible.

And yet, she realized that she carried the blood of Salema, who had done exactly that.

"Do you feel unwell, Your Highness?"

"...No, I'm fine. Please continue, Claudius."

He hesitated slightly but started again when he saw how Falanya look at him head-on.

"Galea ascended to the throne and pardoned his brother after the war. Salema had been destined for execution, but he was allowed to go into exile instead. He washed up on no-man's-land, gathered a group of his loyal followers from his homeland, and established the Kingdom of Natra."

"...Did Galea know why Salema did what he did?"

"According to his notes, it seems they had discussed it before-hand. The truth is: Natra was secretly established with Naliavene's support. There is no question the two were coconspirators."

"I see," Falanya responded before letting out a sigh. "I have mixed feelings about this..."

"It was not what Salema wished for. But at times, being royalty can mean making difficult choices."

"But I could never do that."

"Then what would you have done in this situation, Princess Falanya?"

"I..." She was at a loss for words.

Uncontrollable factions. A father-king standing in the way. Encroaching foreign enemies.

What would she do in this situation?

There was one thing. Just one. The most obvious action that she could take.

"—I'd talk about it with Wein!" she declared.

Even Claudius was surprised by this, blinking back at her with wide eyes. Moments later, he let out a loud guffaw.

"I see. When you're that resolute, I cannot help but commend you. I'm certain Prince Wein would have an idea to turn everything on its head, even in such a difficult predicament."

"Of course he would. He *is* my big brother, after all." Falanya puffed out her chest as if bragging about herself.

Right then, the distant sounds of a commotion filtered through the window.

"Ah!" Falanya rushed over to the sill, spotting a group on horseback in front of the palace. "Um, Claudius," she started, turning back to him.

The elderly instructor nodded. "Very well. It is a little early, but let us end here for today."

"Thank you!" Before he finished his sentence, Falanya had already flown out of the room.

Gathering the hem of her skirt, she pattered down the hallway. Along the way, the eyes of the vassals and court ladies widened at the sight of the princess barreling through, but she paid them no mind.

She knew they were returning today. That's why she had trouble sleeping the night before. As her heart pounded against her chest, she finally reached the entrance hall where the group had now gathered. Falanya picked out one of them.

"Ninym!" she shouted.

Waving in reply was a white-haired girl with red eyes—Ninym Ralei. She was a vassal who served the royal family, but Falanya thought of her more as an older sister.

"Oh my, Princess Falanya. To be personally greeted by you. I'm delighted." Ninym fell to one knee and smiled.

"Come on, Ninym. I'm just happy you're home. That aside—"

"I understand. Over that way." Ninym pointed.

Falanya followed her finger, spotting a boy who was deep in

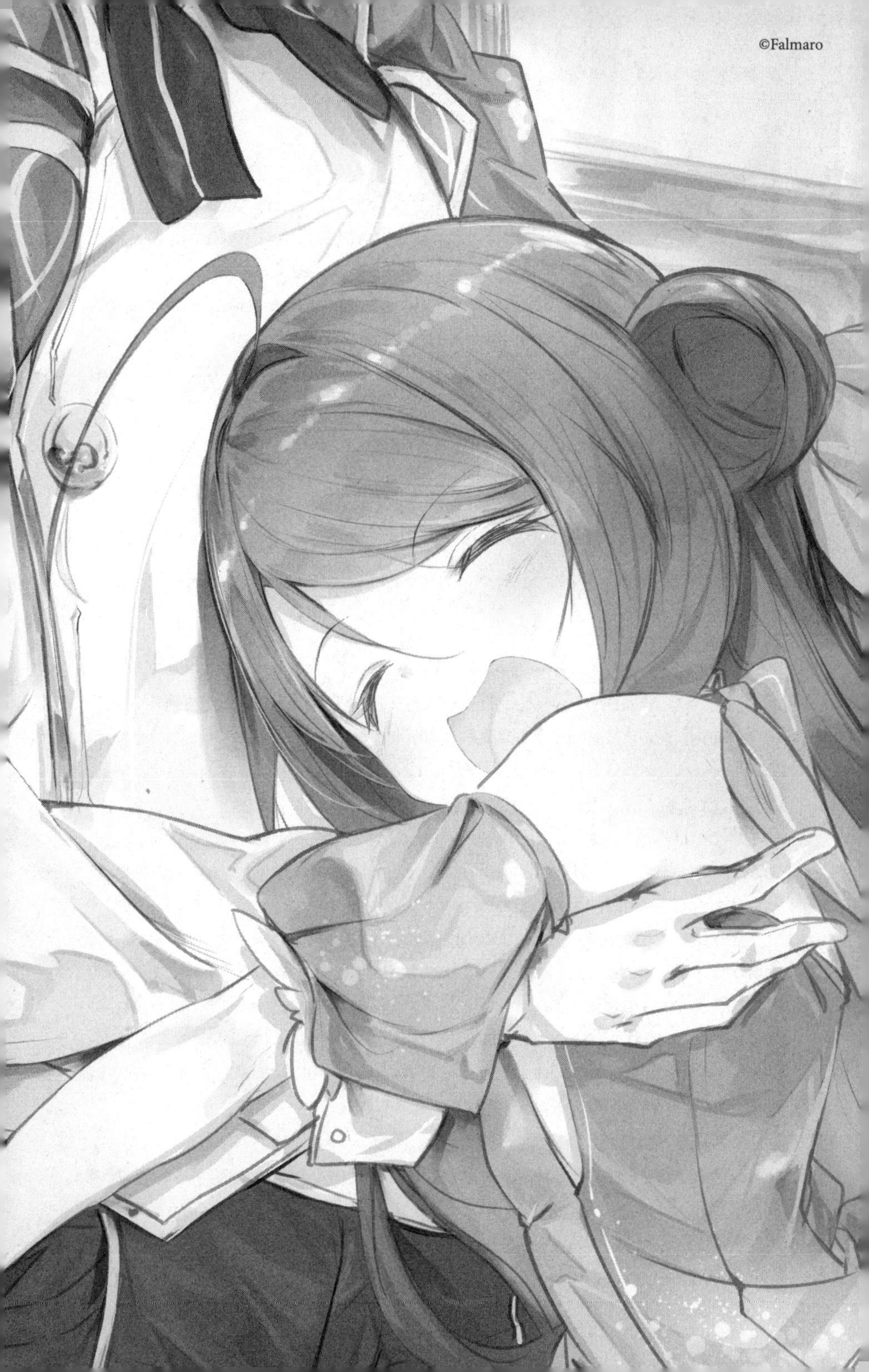

conversation with a small crowd. He was slightly older than her, someone whom she held in high regard and trusted with her life.

The crown prince of the Natra, Wein Salema Arbalest.

"Wein!" she squealed, leaping into his arms as soon as she spotted him.

"Whoa—" He caught her, swinging around in a full circle from the momentum before gently placing her feet back on the floor. He flashed her a smile.

"I'm home, Falanya."

"Welcome back. I'm relieved to see you're well."

As he stroked her hair, Falanya's eyes closed—finally content.

"Let's tour the kingdom over the winter."

The end of summer was when Wein had first brought up this idea.

"We'll visit the territory of each vassal and set up fresh opportunities to talk with them. This is the time to secure a solid base of support, especially when I'm taking over for the king."

When Wein was appointed regent, he'd gone to greet most of the notable figures of Natra. But that hadn't been enough for both parties to gauge each other's character.

As the crown prince, Wein needed to prepare far in advance before he made any public appearances, a process that usually included an official statement. If he made an impulsive decision to set out at the beginning of winter, it would create problems for both the departing team and receiving parties. That was why it was never *too* early to start thinking about these things.

Except for one problem.

"Why pick the time of year when there's gonna be a bunch of snow?"

Ninym had a point. As the northernmost nation on the continent, winter in Natra was brutal. Of course, its residents had grown accustomed to the climate over the years, but that didn't mean they found the snow any easier to travel in. After all, it wasn't as though they could spread their wings and fly.

But Wein had his own reasons.

"We have to keep an eye on our neighbors, which means our only opportunity to make the rounds will be during the winter."

In the East, the Empire had become unstable, leaving the entire continent in a state of disarray. As the link between East and West, Natra had to be vigilant of its surroundings. The speed of its response to an emergency hinged entirely on the prince regent's presence at the palace. Ninym could understand why Wein would insist on touring the provinces in winter, when movements of neighboring nations would be grinding down to a crawl.

"Of course, I know that it'll be hard for us to travel through the snow. But I think the effort of pushing through to meet with the lords of the realm will leave a good impression."

Wein flashed his most princely smile, but Ninym looked at him skeptically.

"Okay, Goody Two-Shoes—what's your real motive?"

"To see if these guys are planning to rebel with my own two eyes…!"

There it is. Ninym sighed, looking up at the ceiling. "But there hasn't been talk of any rebellions, right?"

"Exactly. Think about it. Our feudal system has been holding Natra together for two hundred years. It would be plain weird if they *didn't* try to pull a fast one on us when there's a major shift in power."

The feudal system was based on the principle that a monarch divided territory among various vassals. In return, they would pay taxes and answer calls to arms. Natra was one of many nations on the Varno continent that had adopted this system. But this style of rule came with its own set of dangers.

In many cases, landed vassals were permitted to raise personal retinues. These forces were nominally supposed to supplement the monarch's armies in times of war and maintain order in each vassal's individual domain. On the flip side, it also gave them the necessary tools to defy sovereign rule.

Naturally, most rulers had more soldiers than their vassals, which meant the nobles couldn't really rebel at a moment's notice. Plus, there was the whole issue of biting the hand that fed you.

But as the years went by, and the land was inherited by new heirs, all that history about receiving the land from the monarch began to fade from living memory. With the monarch's influence and the military might of the kingdom in decline, it was natural for vassals to want to seize the opportunity to secure more for themselves.

As Wein had said, the Kingdom of Natra's two-hundred-year history was the longest in the entire continent, and the noble families had lived on their lands for generations. With the current king ill, his replacement a young prince, and a recent war with another nation weakening the kingdom's troops, the vassals were only growing bolder.

"I mean, if I were in their shoes, I'd make sure *something* was done…!" Wein declared.

Ninym sighed. "But I can't imagine there's anyone else in this country like you."

From her perspective, he was just overthinking things.

Of course, she knew there were vassals who did not think highly of Wein. Ever since he was appointed regent, he'd been getting involved in all kinds of business, inevitably running a few nobles off from their positions and livelihoods. At the same time, his balance as a politician was impeccable. Wein always took care not to oppose key influencers while pursuing his vision in national politics. The nobles that did hold a grudge against him were the ones without much clout.

Meanwhile, Wein was popular among his troops—especially with a victory against Marden under his belt. Even though his forces had yet to make a complete recovery, the number of people in the nation with guts to openly oppose Wein had to be paltry.

It'd be a different story if a competent leader took the reins and gathered the disgruntled nobles together, but we're on good terms with those people. Without power, even the most antagonistic nobles choose obedience.

If nothing else, Ninym was fairly certain that a large-scale revolt wasn't on the horizon anytime soon. She wasn't against the idea of Wein touring the kingdom. It was important for rulers to connect with their vassals. It wasn't unprecedented for a hated king's cries for help to go unheeded. Moreover, even though he was in line for the throne, Wein was still young. Going out of his way to meet with the big shots would make a good impression.

Ninym thought she had it all figured out. But Wein was barking up a totally different tree.

"Those opposed to me will probably want to take advantage of our visits and try to assassinate me. We'll have to prepare escape routes ahead of time. While we're at it, how about we scrap most of our guard detail? If we play it right, we'll be justified in crushing 'em…"

"Okay, but why would you go out of your way to stir the pot as a decoy?"

"Hey, c'mon, Ninym. Think about it. If I use myself, I can reel in the rebels without spending any extra cash, right? And once I squash them, my rule will be rock-solid. I can't think of a single reason *not* to do it."

"……" Ninym heaved another sigh.

On a related note, the Empire's Imperial Princess Lowellmina had recently come to Wein, using herself as bait in an attempt to start a rebellion in Imperial territory and failing spectacularly. Ninym had hit the nail on the head when she'd first assessed they were two peas in a pod.

"In conclusion, I think we should start making moves. Ninym, I trust you to handle all prep."

"…Fine, I'll go along with it. But don't come crying to me when things don't go the way you planned. Deal?"

"Oh, *relax*. I'll get those rebels good."

Wein was brimming with confidence.

Returning to the present, the royal tour had just come to a close.

"Everyone with their friggin' poker faces! This is unbelievable!"

Sure enough, Wein was found wailing in his office in Willeron Palace as Ninym stood beside him. After parting with Falanya, he had peeled himself out of his travel clothes, quickly bathed, and squeezed in a quick meeting with his vassals. Now here he was.

"I tried to warn you." Ninym shrugged as she watched Wein squirm in agony.

"What the heck?! Where's your motivation?! This was your big chance, guys! If not now, then when?! This is the part where you step up! Take charge! Forge your own path!"

"Why? That's simple. This country isn't worth rebelling over."

"Gack!"

"If anything, it's too much work for a loss in profits."

"Gugh!"

"It's easier to leave the boring tasks to you, kick back, and collect an easy paycheck."

"NOOOOOOOOOOO!" Wein shrieked.

Ninym posed a basic question. "Were you that eager for a rebellion?"

"I don't want one at all! But I would be lying if I said I wasn't hoping for a minor rebellion that's easy to suppress and gives us grounds to seize their fortunes—to fill the country's coffers!"

"Ah yes. A perfectly egotistical plan."

Even Ninym could only feel exasperated by her master's rotten nature.

"Well, in any case, now we know. All the powerful nobles you paid a visit to are supportive, and there are no known rumors of opposition brewing. Even if some are unsatisfied, there isn't a single person in Natra with the strength to overthrow you at this moment."

Ninym was right. Wein had been warmly welcomed in many of the territories they had visited. Certainly, they had their own motives and goals for supporting him. But the majority were ready to hop aboard Wein's ship.

"Uuuugh! I toiled through hardship and braved the snow, and *this* is what I get…? I won't give up. Plan B has to work."

Wein's plan to travel to each area with a small guard detail to invite open rebellion had failed. But Wein had another scheme ready in his back pocket.

"I'm sure that one will face the same fate."

"Hey, that's not true! I think! I know! I hope…" He trailed off, thinking about his last failure before face-planting on his desk.

"…I'm suddenly exhausted."

"I knew your plot was destined to fail. But that doesn't change the fact that touring the kingdom in the winter was tough. You can relax now; we're back safe and sound. We should go to bed early tonight."

"No kidding… Whose idea was it to do this during winter anyway?"

"Yours, Wein."

"Oh yeah…" Wein moaned weakly from the desk. "Wait; this is bad. I forgot this was the work zone. Why am I relaxing in here? Makes me seem like a workaholic…"

"I don't see anything wrong with that."

"It's terrible!" Wein shouted, sitting up emphatically from his desk. "If I keep this up, I'll become an uptight square who looks for work in retirement—even after I finish selling out the country! I should be…living the lazy life, starting right now!"

"I see…"

"What's this? C'mon now. What's with that attitude? I bet you're thinking *Here he goes again, spouting the same ol' bull.* I'll have you know that I'm gonna follow through! I totally will!"

"With what time and money?"

"……" Wein banged his head on the desk.

"I'm certain your legacy will live on as a beautiful tale."

"Yeah, they'll remember me as the supreme hot genius prince…"

"'Hot' is pushing it."

"I'll never understand why you're so hard on my looks, Miss Ninym…"

"As your servant, it is only natural."

That's definitely not natural.

But as soon as that thought crossed Wein's mind, there was a knock at the office door before it was thrown open.

"Wein, Ninym, may I come in now?"

"—Of course. I'm sorry to have kept you waiting, Falanya."

His change in demeanor could truly be considered an expert performance. Wein adopted the air of a capable young scion as he greeted Falanya. Ninym flashed him a look: *Damn show-off.* He ignored it with grace.

"How were things while we were away, Falanya? Anything odd happen?"

"Everything was the same as always. I listened to Claudius's lectures; I played with Nanaki; I ate Holly's pancakes—"

Falanya started to rattle off occurrences in her daily life. Wein and Ninym listened carefully, occasionally interjecting to make appropriate comments. From this conversation, they gathered that she was beloved by many who served the palace.

"—That sounds nice. I'm relieved to hear everything was good at home." Wein stroked Falanya's hair when she finished, and she broke into a contented smile.

"How did things go for you, Wein?"

"We were able to meet everyone as planned and assess conditions in each of the provinces. The outcome was better than expected."

"That's just what I'd expect from you," Falanya praised before sulking. "You could have come home sooner, though."

"Come now. Don't be like that, Falanya. We tried to pack in as much as possible in the little time we had. Right, Ninym?"

"Precisely. It's inevitable that traveling in the winter takes time. Curtailing our trip any further would have proved difficult."

"Grr. You're taking his side, Ninym?" Falanya puffed up her cheeks. "Why do you have to go out to greet people in the first place, Wein? You're the prince regent. They should be summoned to the palace instead."

"That's exactly why. I'm in a position where I can call upon others. If I go out myself, I honor the other person."

He had actually been trying to lure out rebels, but he could never tell her that. If he did, his sister would definitely get angry and say he was terrible for doubting his vassals.

Well, she's cute when she's mad, too, Wein thought.

I suppose he has a point, Falanya acquiesced.

The siblings nodded at each other at the same time.

"Hmm, I see."

Based on her expression, Wein could see it was clear that Falanya reluctantly accepted his answer. That was only natural since it wasn't sound logic that was most important to her but her big brother's affections.

Wein knew this, and it made him smile.

"Don't worry, Falanya. I'll be stuck in the palace for a while, recovering from this trip. I promise to make up for all the lonely moments that you endured."

"Really?" Falanya's eyes sparkled.

"Of course. Well, it's getting late. You should head back to your room for the night."

Her mood immediately turned dour. "What? But even the moon is out playing with the stars."

"No dice. I heard you didn't sleep yesterday. I bet you're tired right now."

"Urgh…"

Wein's pointed observation left her speechless. In all honesty, sheep were already crowding the back of her mind as bedtime drew near.

"I plan on turning in early, too. Ninym will see you off."

"Well, let us get going, Princess Falanya."

"Hmph… Remember your promise, Wein. You can't forget."

"Yes, of course. I wouldn't lie to you."

Falanya had no argument. She pouted and left the room with Ninym.

All alone, Wein spoke to himself.

"—Well…"

It would be spring in Natra soon. On the southern end of the continent, the winter season had already departed, meaning all the nations of the land were beginning to buzz with activity once again.

"…That's only if nothing happens," Wein murmured, hoping for the best.

Of course, there was no way his wish could be granted.

"An emissary from Cavarin?"

Just as it seemed like they'd finally recovered from their long journey, taken care of miscellaneous matters, and resumed business as usual, the announcement came.

"Yes, they arrived moments ago. It appears they have an official message from the king of Cavarin," Ninym added.

Wein folded his arms as he considered this news. Cavarin was a nation bordering Natra to the west. They had only become neighbors the previous year. Before that, the territory had been a nation known as Marden.

But during the Natra–Marden War over the gold mine, Cavarin troops had attacked and conquered the former royal capital of Marden, Tholituke. With most of the royal family captured and executed, Marden was no more, making Natra and Cavarin new neighbors. But with only a nonaggression pact to define their relationship, both kingdoms fell into a vague diplomatic situation that was neither friendly nor hostile.

There were reasons for this. Natra was busy running its new gold mine and negotiating deals with the Empire in the East, while Cavarin's occupation was met with resistance by the Marden army. Both kingdoms had their hands full thinking about this sort of thing.

"Hmm. I'm guessing this official letter isn't a declaration of war."

"What do you want to do? Sending someone else to receive them instead of going yourself is an option."

"No, I'll go. I don't know how much this emissary knows, but I want to dig for leads."

"Understood. I'll arrange a meeting. Before that, there is one thing about the emissary…"

As Wein had ordered, an appointment was set. Since the Cavarin delegation hailed from the West, there were no Flahm in the room—including Ninym. Accompanied by his guards, Wein headed to the room where a man reminiscent of a reedy, withering tree waited for him.

"—It is my pleasure to meet you, Prince Regent," the man announced with a masterful bow and a thick voice that almost seemed viscous. "My name is Holonyeh. I am but a single servant of the king of Cavarin. I have come to your nation on his behalf."

Holonyeh. Wein gave no reaction upon hearing the name. After all, Ninym had told him beforehand.

"We warmly welcome you, Lord Holonyeh." Wein nodded, gazing at him intently. "Before discussing the subject at hand, there's something I'd like to ask. Didn't you serve the Kingdom of Marden? Or is my memory failing me?"

"Oh, dear me." Holonyeh smiled rather than appearing shaken. "As perceptive as the rumors claim… I'm in awe. You are right; I was indeed in the pay of Marden. But after the nation collapsed, and I found myself at a loss, I was appointed to a new position by the ruler of Cavarin, King Ordalasse."

"And then you rose up to become the emissary of a neighboring nation. Not one to miss an opportunity, I see," Wein added sarcastically.

"It is all thanks to the great King Ordalasse." Holonyeh only bowed his head reverently.

I guess anyone who would take such obvious bait would never get hired in the first place.

Wein had taken a jab at Holonyeh to get a feel for his character, but it was a wasted effort. He switched gears and decided to get to the heart of the matter.

"Lord Holonyeh, I gather you're here on some kind of mission for King Ordalasse?"

"Indeed. I ask that you look at this."

He presented a sealed letter with the crest of Cavarin carved into the wax. Inside was a single sheet with King Ordalasse's signature at the bottom. There was no questioning its authenticity. As Wein read it, his eyes widened.

"Lord Holonyeh… Is this real?"

"Yes. I have a message from the king, as well." Holonyeh paused before continuing. "In order to deepen the friendship between the kingdoms of Natra and Cavarin, the king wishes to invite you, Prince Regent, to attend our Festival of the Spirit held at the royal capital—"

A few days had passed since the arrival of Cavarin's emissary.

"Invited to the Festival of the Spirit, huh?" Falanya groaned as she toyed with a feather quill.

She had heard about the meeting between Wein and the emissary. Her main takeaway was that her beloved big brother would be going on another trip, but—

"Hey, Claudius. You're from the West, right? Do you know about the Festival of the Spirit?"

"Why, of course." The tutor nodded as he carried on his lesson in a new direction. "Do you know the Teachings of Levetia, Princess?"

"It's a famous religion in the West, I think?"

Levetia was a monotheistic religion established a few hundred years prior. It had a particularly strong hold in the West.

"That should be enough context. The Festival of the Spirit is a Levetian ritual held in early spring. It began when the founder, Levetia—with the protection of God—freed the masses from the demons torturing them. It is now celebrated as a day to express gratitude for the great feat. As a matter of fact, there are devotees throughout Natra who participate in their own events." Claudius cracked a small smile.

"Naturally," he continued, "the general purpose of the festival is to celebrate the coming of spring. Honoring Levetia is for the most pious of believers."

"I gather Cavarin is inviting Wein to this festival to become better friends with Natra?"

"Well, I'm merely a humble instructor. It is rather difficult for me to answer that question," he replied, shaking his head. "If I could bring up one point of concern, it is that the Festival of the Spirit in the royal capital takes place at the same time as the Gathering of the Chosen this year."

"The Gathering of the Chosen?" Falanya tilted her head.

"The Holy King is the head of Levetia, and those who serve under him as assistants are called the Holy Elites. The Holy King is chosen from among them. You could also say the Holy Elites are candidates for the Holy King."

Claudius drew a simple triangle. *Holy King* was written at the very top with *Holy Elites* on the level directly beneath it, followed by *Priests* and *Believers*.

"The Holy King and the Elites meet once a year. This is called the Gathering of the Chosen."

Falanya considered this new information for a few moments. "Is it a very important meeting?"

Claudius nodded. "Indeed. The Teachings of Levetia is the most prominent religion in the West. In addition to the Holy King and Elites, there will be an array of other rulers and influential figures in attendance. This gathering might be considered the largest international conference in the West."

"Ah, and it'll take place in Cavarin, which means..."

"Correct. King Ordalasse is one of the Holy Elites."

The location of the gathering changed each year on a rotational basis, always hosted in an Elite's city of residence. This year, it would be held in Cavarin's royal capital alongside the Festival of the Spirit.

"...Wein showed me the letter, but it didn't say anything about the Gathering of the Chosen. Just that he was invited to the festival."

Falanya moaned once again. "I wonder what their king could be planning?"

"There must be some motive. Especially since it cannot be said that the Holy Elites have no relation with Prince Wein...or rather, with the royal family of Natra."

"What do you mean?"

"The relationship between the Holy King and the Holy Elites began with the founder, Levetia, and the lead disciples. To become an Elite, one must carry the blood of Levetia or one of the followers..."

Falanya understood what he was getting at. "...Which means our family..."

"Yes. As a member of the royal family in Naliavene, our founder, Salema, is descended from an ancient bloodline related to Levetia's disciple, Galeus."

In other words, his descendants—including Wein and Falanya—fulfilled one of the conditions required to become a Holy Elite.

Falanya never realized she had this blood coursing through her veins in addition to being royalty. She stared, fixated, at her hands.

"Of course, that only satisfies a single requirement. Any who truly wish to become a Holy Elite would need assets, military power, political clout, and a number of other things."

"......"

The Festival of the Spirit and the Gathering of the Chosen. It was obvious that Cavarin had invited Wein—a possible Elite—with hidden intentions in mind. Falanya couldn't imagine what they could be, but they had to pose a danger to Wein.

"I wonder what Wein will do..."

This was a matter of national politics. As she was now, she had no right to interfere. That said, she wanted Wein to stay home for as long as possible. Falanya held on to these thoughts with concern for her brother, all the while wishing they could stay together.

*   *   *

————Meanwhile.

"I DON'T WANNA GOOOOOOOO!" Wein screamed in his office. "BUT I GOTTA!"

"I knew this would happen," Ninym said at his side as he cradled his head in his hands. "The timing is perfect. There's nothing weird about inviting you to the festival. With spring just over the horizon, of course they'd be thinking about reexamining our unstable relationship."

"…Don't you think there's a possibility they're calling me out to set up an assassination?"

"I can't rule it out. But that would just provoke Natra into declaring war. With Cavarin already trying to deal with the remnants of Marden's army, it would mean fighting on multiple fronts. Wouldn't it be more strategic for them to seek cooperation by strengthening our alliance?"

"Yeah, you're right. If it had been any other year, I swear I would have honestly thought the same thiiiiiiiing!"

Ninym nodded. "It's worth noting that this meeting coincides with the Gathering of the Chosen at their royal capital. Of course, it could merely be a total scheduling coincidence…"

"There's no way. My guess is that it's a ploy to have me join the Holy Elites. I mean, it's pretty much a de facto political faction."

"With your accomplishments and pedigree, they're probably considering you as a future Elite… They must be hoping to properly evaluate you. They'll want to establish the pecking order while they still can."

Of course, this was just a theory. But in either case, the greatest powerhouse of the West was expecting him. There was no way he could duck out with a quick greeting.

"If I go, I'll definitely get caught up in some kind of trouble."

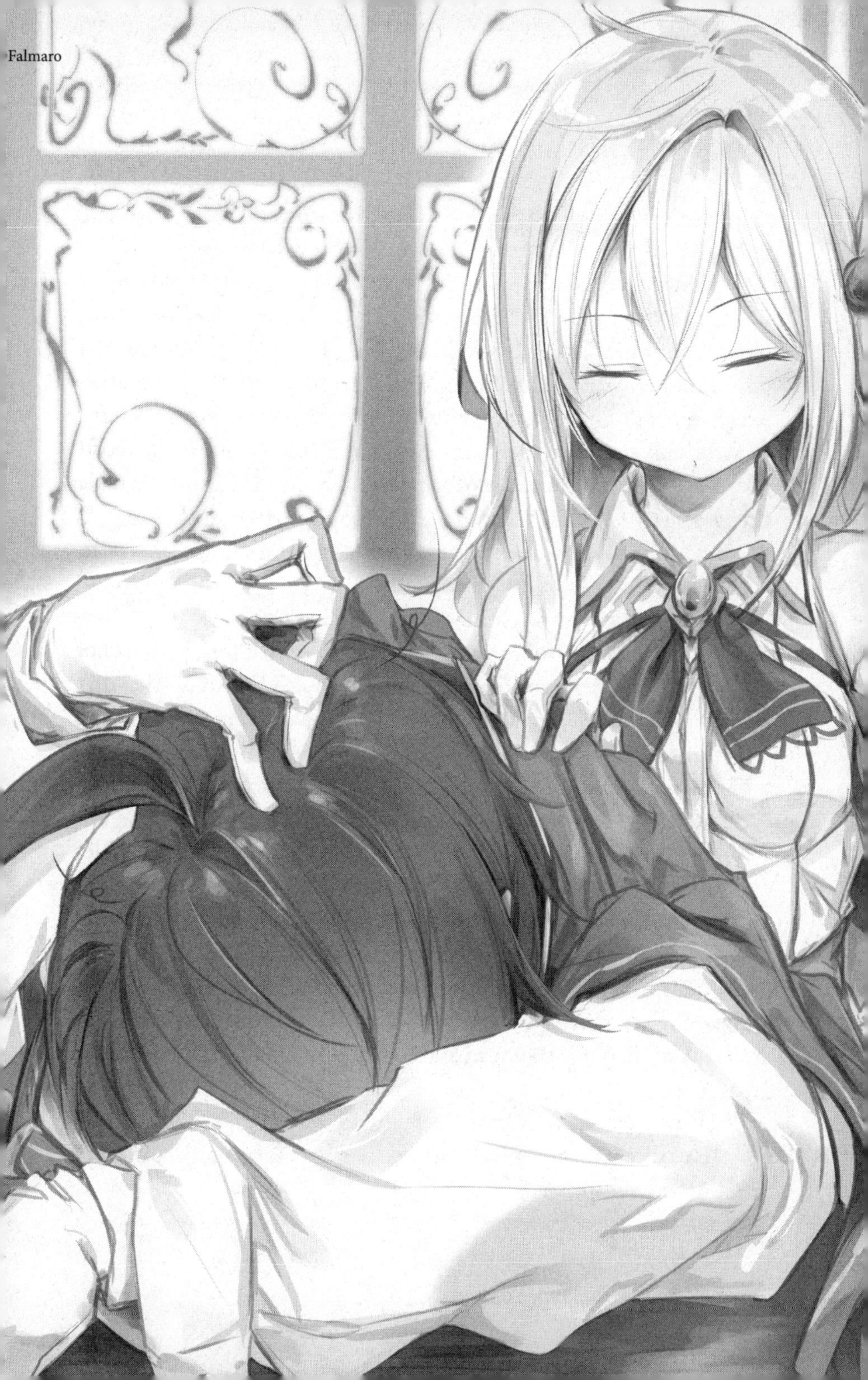
Falmaro

"I don't doubt it." Ninym nodded. "But it would be unfortunate to let this chance at improving relations with the West slip by."

"Yeah, you've got a point…" He trailed off. "Aaaah! Why?!" Wein unleashed his anguish. "I know we've got a trade-dependent economy… But our relationship with the West has been on hold for the past hundred years. Teaming up with Cavarin could be huge for us! And if everything works out, our country's value will soar!"

After all, their founder had anticipated this barren land would become a bustling hub connecting the East and West. Although the northern lands had various disadvantages, they still managed to flourish until those hundred years of deteriorating relations with the West.

"Then, I take that you'll accept their invitation?"

He had been personally invited by the king himself. If Wein wanted a direct conversation, he had no choice but to go there. A pained look crossed his face for a moment as he thought things over, but ultimately he nodded.

"…Yeah, let's do it. We can't tell what the other side is thinking with our limited information. I don't *think* they'll try to kill me. I'm gonna jump right in."

"Things are going to get busy again, even though we only got back to the palace just the other day."

"No kidding… Why am I working so much…?"

"Because you're the crown prince of Natra, obviously," Ninym quipped, giving the slouched Wein a side-glance. She turned on her heel. "Well then, I'll go ahead and prepare a schedule. I'll leave other matters to you, Wein."

"'Other matters'? …Oh right, replying to the letter."

"That, too; but there's something else even more important."

"Care to remind me?"

"Apologizing to Falanya."

"Oomph…"

Wein looked up at the ceiling and seriously despaired over what he should tell his little sister now that he had to break his promise to spend time together.

Fate had already begun weaving a new tale.

Heralded by the death of the Earthworld's Emperor, this era became known as the Great War of Kings. The chance meeting between Wein Salema Arbalest and the Holy Elites would give rise to chaos across the Western continent.

A delegation to send to the royal capital in Cavarin was hastily pieced together.

After all, Cavarin couldn't be reached in a day or two. That meant they had to decide on a route, find lodgings along the way, gather their entourage, and prepare the necessary provisions. On top of it all, they had to align themselves with Western culture.

"Ninym, I'm going to Cavarin by carriage. Go ahead and bring it out."

"Really? All right, but carriages are typically for women."

"In the East. Especially in the Empire."

The Empire was a meritocracy, where riding on horseback was a symbol of strength. There, it would be ridiculous for royals and noblemen to use carriages. Others would point and laugh that they couldn't ride a horse without training wheels.

"There's an understanding in the West that nobles shouldn't excessively be in the public eye. If a royal was to ride in on a horse unaided, they'd be seen as a foreign barbarian. At least, that's what Claudius told me."

"I see. I'll have it ready."

"I'm leaving that to you. I have to go review Western etiquette with Claudius… They're a stiff crowd."

The delegation's preparations to head West proceeded steadily— until a certain issue arose.

"Prince Regent, I'm terribly sorry, but might you cut a few more people from your party?" Holonyeh asked. "The Holy Elites will be attending the Festival of the Spirit, which means the royal capital will be more congested than we expected."

In other words, they'd hit max capacity.

Even under the best circumstances, a festival brought in local crowds. Add in Wein and the Holy Elites, and it wasn't hard to see why Cavarin would have a hard time finding lodging for everyone.

But Wein had an objection.

"I unfortunately can't make it any less than fifty. It'll cause trouble for my guards."

After all, this was an age where bandits were liable to crop up as soon as they left behind civilization. It had been that way while they were out on the royal tour, and there was no way Wein could walk around without any guards.

Even from a power perspective, it was important for people to accompany him. If his retinue was too small, people would wonder if that was all the crown prince of Natra could afford. But if he went overboard, his peers would be intimidated, fretting that he was coming to declare war and becoming hypervigilant. With this in mind, Wein had settled on fifty and showed no intention of backing down.

Holonyeh eventually acquiesced, so his delegation stayed intact. The emissary returned to Cavarin ahead of time to relay Wein's answer, while Wein plugged away at his overdue work and wrestled over how to put Falanya in a good mood.

Two weeks after Holonyeh made his return, everything was in order, and they were at last ready to depart.

Wein was now in a carriage headed for Cavarin.

"——I'm honestly shocked."

Soldiers in his retinue were stationed on all sides, and gaudy ornamentation adorned the carriage. Anyone could tell their group belonged to a noble.

"About what?" Ninym asked as she sat across from him. Wein reached toward her.

"Your hair." Wein ran his fingers through a tuft of it.

"Ah." She touched it in understanding.

——It was black.

Ninym's head of snowy hair had been dyed the color of night.

"You know that the Flahm are masters of disguise, right? I'm not as good as Nanaki, but I can do at least this much."

They were heading toward the Kingdom of Cavarin in the west, where racial prejudice ran deep. In particular, the Flahm were scorned. Wein had questioned whether to bring along Ninym, who was both his close aide and a Flahm.

Cavarin had to have their own unique ways of thinking. And Wein wanted Ninym nearby to give him advice. Ninym herself had no objections.

But it would cause unnecessary trouble for her to appear as a Flahm. Hence this solution: Ninym dyed her hair.

"I can't change my eye color, but as long as no one pays close attention, they won't realize I'm a Flahm."

"You had me fooled. I couldn't even tell it was dyed."

"That's because this is a secret trick of the Flahm people." Then, with a dyed head of hair, Ninym flashed Wein a mischievous grin, pressing him for his opinion. "Oh, Wein. By the way, do you think I look better with white or black?"

"Oh, there it is. Right here, right now. I already know you'll get all huffy whichever one I pick."

"Oh, and by the way, it'll come back to bite you if you try to get out of it by teasing me."

"……" He'd been cornered. With some difficulty, Wein considered all options before coming to a conclusion.

"———White!"

Oh-ho, Ninym's face seemed to say.

"It's rare for you to be this resolute."

"Hey now, Ninym, I am an honest prince who upholds a creed of decisiveness."

"Yeah, yeah. Hmm. White, huh?" Ninym took a lock in her hand and gently dabbed her eyes. "And to think that I dyed it black just for you. You're breaking my heart."

"There it is, dammit! That's not fair!"

"'Not fair,' my butt. It's a totally normal reaction for a woman."

"Yeah? Then I've got something else to say. Listen up, Ninym! Yeah, you asked me if I preferred black or white, but you never specified that it was about your hair! In other words!"

"'In other words'?"

"I was talkin' about underwear. —*Bweh.*"

Ninym's fist had sunk deep into Wein's cheek.

"Well, I might have gotten carried away, too. Let's strike a deal."

"I'm sure I've been struck enough for the day."

"To make up for your pain, you can touch my hair as much as you like… Oh, but not too hard. The color will come out."

Rub, rub, rub.

"Hey! I *just* said don't do that! It'll be difficult to redo this, you know!"

Wein laughed and let go as Ninym snarled at him with bared teeth. She jabbed a finger at the tip of his nose.

"And, Wein, I'm warning you right now that you can't be reckless once we're in Cavarin. Even if you don't agree with their culture and ideologies, you can't go flying off the handle. I'll stay in the background and hide away indoors as much as possible."

"Okay, okay, I know. I'm not that stupid."

"Then can you promise me?"

"Sure. Have I ever broken a promise before?"

"All the time."

"…Guess we just have to have faith in the future me!"

"If you break your promise, I'll stuff a potato in every orifice of your body."

"It's not very good to waste food…!"

Their conversation carried on in this fashion until a knock came from outside the carriage window. The two turned to see Raklum next to them on horseback.

Raklum was a commander in the army of Natra who had sworn loyalty to Wein. Though still young, he was excellent in battle and was a capable leader, which was why he had been entrusted with overseeing the delegation.

"Your Highness, I apologize for interrupting. We will soon be arriving at the Jilaat gold mine, and I wish to give my report."

"Oh, we're finally here."

Last year, Natra had seized the Jilaat gold mine after a war with Marden. They had been under the impression that the reserves had dwindled, but they discovered a new pocket of gold, making it one of Natra's most crucial holdings.

"The locals have been given advance notice, and they should be ready to receive us. I think we should rest at the foot of the mine as planned tonight."

"Understood. I'll leave it to you."

"Very good, Your Highness." Raklum distanced himself from the carriage.

The journey from Natra to Cavarin was a long one. It couldn't be done in a day, which was why they had decided on a number of rest stops. The foot of the gold mine was one of them.

"Wein, keep in mind that there's supposed to be a banquet and a meeting upon arrival."

"Got it. With who?"

"Supervisor Pelynt and General Hagal. We have no plans to enter the fortress in front of the gold mine, so we'll be meeting them there."

"Hagal, huh? …I see. Perfect timing. There's something else I want to talk about with him."

Ninym nodded. "Don't forget the banquet. As a politician, it's important that you show the people your good side."

"I know, I know. Besides, if I pass this opportunity up, who knows when I'll be able to eat Natran food again. I plan on enjoying it while I can."

The delegation slowly continued winding its way to the foot of the mine.

"We have been expecting you, Prince Wein."

The local magistrate of the Jilaat gold mine—a man named Pelynt—greeted the delegation at the base of the mountain. He had originally been a vassal of Marden but spent his days in exile, toiling as a miner after losing a political battle. But when Wein had showed up with his forces to capture the mine, he had noticed Pelynt and appointed him as a local magistrate.

"Thanks for coming to meet us." Wein climbed out of the carriage and offered his gratitude with a wry smile. "Who knew we'd be see-ing each other again so soon. Sorry for imposing on you like this."

Wein had actually stayed at the gold mine during his winter vis-its. They had thrown a huge banquet then, too, which was why he was feeling bad about showing up again so quickly.

"I'm obliged by your generous words, but please have no fear. There is no one here who would be unhappy to welcome the prince who saved our lives. You can make all the visits in the world. It may be modest, but we have prepared a feast for you. Please, right this way."

Guided by Pelynt, Wein set off with Ninym and his guards.

...Things really have changed around here.

Wein noted their surroundings. It was now a prospering town, far better than what it had been like before.

Since coming under Natra's rule, the lives of the people working in the gold mine had improved drastically. This could all be attributed to Wein's policies. Once known for its squalid environment and harsh working conditions, the mine had claimed the lives of many of its laborers, which Wein had deemed unacceptable. Instead of treating people as disposable beasts of burden, Wein had made it a priority to provide them with sufficient safety, homes, food, and pay. He considered mining as only a part of their work, earning enough respect to access their knowledge and experience.

Of course, there were other motivations at play, too. It would have been a big pain if they rebelled due to mistreatment. And he'd given off a philanthropic vibe that he couldn't back out on anymore. In any case, the people of the mine had welcomed his new policies with open arms.

They had set to work, roused by the need to meet Prince Wein's expectations. Some were more than happy to try to slack off, but Wein—who was lazier than most—had anticipated this and put strict ordinances in place to keep that to a minimum.

The mine had begun to buzz with energy, and people from the surrounding area started to stream in as word spread. As the population grew, the merchants with the sharpest eyes showed up. The miners lavished them with generous profits, and it wasn't long before more people realized they could make a killing here. Next to arrive were craftsmen as the townspeople demanded more homes and sundries—and before anyone realized it, the Jilaat gold mine had become a bustling mining town.

"I know I asked last time, but have there been any changes to the mine itself, Pelynt?"

"Yes. The equipment and tunnels damaged during the war have been repaired. Since we have more hands available now, the excavation has been proceeding very smoothly. At present, we have begun to search for new pockets of gold along with our usual activities."

The gold mine was doing well. That was thrilling news. Inside, Wein grinned sloppily.

"I'm glad to hear it. Don't let management slip from getting too caught up in mining. If you get too many people coming in and out, you'll attract the more unsavory types."

"Yes! I will keep that in mind." Pelynt gave a reverent bow.

As Wein nodded magnanimously, there was a small poke in his ribs.

"Wein, your face."

"Oops."

His face must have slackened upon hearing the news of the mine. With Ninym by his side to rebuke him with a whispered comment, Wein hurriedly composed his expression.

In any case, it would seem the mine is doing well.

Wein couldn't have been happier. It had been well worth it to construct a road connecting the royal capital in Natra to the mine to facilitate the exchange of goods and people.

Thanks to this new road, their carriage had been able to travel to the mine, despite the ground still being slick with snow. It was difficult to predict what decisions could make an impact in the future, but this had been a lucky bet.

Which leaves military preparedness as the primary remaining concern.

In all aspects, the gold mine was drool worthy. If the booming mining town continued to develop, its value would climb even higher. Wein knew there were a number of forces ready to swipe it from under their noses the moment they got a chance. To prevent that, the town would need to strengthen its defenses.

Well, in actuality, Wein was already a step ahead. He had constructed a new defensive fortress to the west of the mine, garrisoned by a top general in Natra, Hagal. Its mission was to hold out against the remaining Marden troops and Cavarin. But with the fortress unfinished, only the bare minimum of soldiers had been stationed there.

"To bring this fortress up to par, we'll need three times the provisions, labor, funds, and time," Hagal had said. And where exactly was Wein going to find all that?

As he thought, the party arrived in front of a noticeably elegant mansion. The structure dated back to when the land was still Marden territory, and it was currently serving as a reception hall and guesthouse for visiting dignitaries.

"By the way, Pelynt, where's Hagal?"

It was an innocent enough question, but Pelynt looked slightly unsettled.

"It seems the general hasn't arrived yet... He must be delayed with administrative tasks..."

"I see. Well, no matter." Wein wasn't particularly bothered by this and headed toward the mansion.

Walking beside him, Wein noticed in secret that Pelynt's profile looked nervous.

At the reception hall, the banquet proceeded smoothly. Wein conversed with the mine residents and merchants as he smacked his lips over the food. Since they'd just had a feast together a short while ago, no one was especially nervous, and the overall atmosphere was inviting.

But right in the middle of it all, a single incident ruined the moods.

Just as the party was in full swing, Hagal made his appearance.

"Your Highness, I apologize for my tardiness. It is I, Hagal."

The old man got down on one knee, and Wein spoke with a wineglass in one hand. "Glad you could make it. But arriving later than me? I think you're getting a little careless."

It was a sharp comment that came directly from the crown prince himself. The people around them knew Wein to be mild mannered and instinctively jolted in nervous shock.

"I have no excuse. I take full responsibility," Hagal apologized as all eyes focused on him.

Wein smiled. "I'm joking. I know you're busy. Here, pull up a chair."

"Of course."

Urged by Wein, Hagal joined the banquet. Wein rebuked him no further, and the others in attendance breathed an internal sigh of relief.

"...Phew."

The party came to an end, and as the evening grew late, Pelynt heaved a heavy sigh in a corner of the mansion. He sighed for two reasons: because the event had concluded without a hitch and to ease his nerves.

"Sir Pelynt," a voice called out behind him.

He turned around to find Raklum standing there.

"Oh, Sir Raklum. I apologize for having you meet me here."

Raklum often accompanied Wein, which was why he had met Pelynt on a few occasions during the war with Marden and the recent royal visits. They'd established a kind of familiar relationship.

"Don't worry about it. There seems to be something you want to ask me. What could it be? Is there a problem with the night guards?"

"No, nothing like that." Pelynt shook his head, though he struggled to get the next words out. He knew it would touch a nerve with Raklum, who had placed his faith in Wein.

"Sir Pelynt?"

"...Please allow me to say that I don't believe this at all of the crown prince regent. But there is something that I must confirm." Even as he sensed the dangerous aura emitting from Raklum, Pelynt continued. "Recently, a certain rumor has been traveling throughout these parts. It began after His Highness's recent visits."

"...And what could that be?"

Pelynt paused for a few seconds, then steeled himself.

"That General Hagal had displeased Prince Wein, and a chasm has opened up between them—"

"...A rift between me and Hagal?"

In a room prepared for them in the mansion, Wein murmured as he sat on a chair.

"Yes. It appears this rumor is spreading across every region," Ninym replied politely as she stood nearby.

A rumor about discord between the crown prince and a prominent military leader. Common sense would say this was a grave issue. If they weren't careful, it might even lead to a large-scale rebellion...

"*Our strategy's* working pretty well, huh, *Hagal?*"

"Indeed." Hagal bowed in reverence. "The plan to spread these rumors to lure dissenters to come together around me so we can round them up all at once... Everything is as you predicted."

That was right. The rumors of bad blood between the two were part of the grand plan that Wein had secretly proposed to Hagal when he came to conduct his winter tour. He figured that even if he was away scouting things out, the rebels wouldn't make a move without a leader. That was where Hagal came in. He was an established military figure, and in a nation where most generals lacked actual battle experience, few had as many achievements as him. He would make an excellent rebel leader. If these rumors spread, the malcontents would try to get in touch with him. At least, that was the idea.

"None have approached me yet, but it will not be long before we see results."

"Right. Be sure to contact me if anything happens."

"Understood."

They chatted for a while longer before Hagal left the room. Wein adopted a look of pure rapture at the progress of his scheme. But Ninym felt otherwise.

"Hey, Wein, are you really going to go forward with this plan?"

"What? Are you against it, Ninym?"

She nodded as if that was obvious. To start, this plan was essentially a fake feud between Wein, the head of the nation, and Hagal, a well-trusted military official. It would incite the rebels—and stir unrest in the nation. Ninym didn't see the merit of going this far to incite a rebellion.

"I know what you mean. I'm still hung up on something I saw when we visited the most suspicious bunch."

"Do you really think they're planning to rebel?"

"That's what I want to confirm. And if it does end up being true, I want to move this plan forward and get the upper hand."

"…Okay, fine. But even then, don't forget to back out if things keep dragging out," Ninym said, stating her honest opinion. "If this plan of yours goes on for too long, you run the risk of hurting General Hagal's reputation. Not to mention that the general was born in a nation that prizes reputation above all else."

To most, reputation was key. But for those whose livelihood was tied to war, it was of utmost importance. They were always dancing with death, which made many of them want to die with a noble legacy, if nothing else.

Plus, Hagal was old. It was natural that he was preoccupied with peace of mind over fleeting worldly gain. Ninym didn't think injuring his reputation was a good idea at all.

"If he gets fed up with you and the deteriorating situation, he might actually rebel."

"Oh, he won't do that. I talked with him while we were out making the rounds. Plus, he's like a grandfather to me and Falanya."

"Which means you're using your grandfather as bait," Ninym retorted.

Wein raised his hands in defeat. "Okay, okay. If time passes, and I'm not making any progress, I'll back out. Deal?"

Ninym nodded. Since the plan was already in motion, this was as good as it was going to get.

Wein had opinions of his own. *She's totally overthinking this*, he grumbled.

"You think I'm overreacting."

"Gah." He didn't even have time to wonder how she'd read his mind.

Ninym tugged Wein's cheek.

"For your information, you're too optimistic. General Hagal is someone you should be treating carefully as it is, but this—"

"No, okay, I get it. I was wrong."

Wein hastily cut off her loud lecture, which was starting to seem very long.

Meanwhile, Hagal had left the mansion after parting with Wein—rather than retire to his room. He gazed at the night sky all alone.

"Ah! So this is where you were, General Hagal."

He turned around to see a woman. "I've seen you somewhere before."

"Yes. I am Ibis the merchant. I have been visiting this town regularly for some time now." She bowed deeply—with grace that didn't appear merchantly at all.

"...And what business do you have with me?"

Ibis responded, "Actually, I have welcome news for Your Excellency."

"Oh? And what might that be?"

At this, Ibis revealed an elegant smile. It was soft and as dark as the void.

"One that will immediately dispel your troubles—"

After leaving the mining town, the delegation passed by the fortress in progress and headed southwest along the highway. Cavarin territory officially began past the fortress, though Wein knew it was a hot point of contention.

"This is a disputed zone between the remnant troops of Marden and the Cavarin forces. Until we enter Cavarin's main sphere of influence, we'll proceed with caution."

"Understood."

Obeying Wein's instructions, the delegation stayed vigilant for the old Marden army.

The royal capital of Marden had fallen to Cavarin's surprise attack during the war with Natra. But Helmut, the second prince of the Marden Kingdom, had escaped, gathering together the soldiers who retreated from the mine to form his own army.

It was commonly referred to as the Remnant Army, though they called themselves the Liberation Front. They fought to retake the royal capital and revive the Kingdom of Marden. That was why they had their spears pointed at Cavarin, still engaged in combat even a year later.

Fortunately for Natra, Cavarin wasn't alone in wanting to avoid a two-front war at all costs. The Remnant Army also hadn't interfered with Natra's efforts to up the mine's defenses.

But stepping into a disputed zone was a different story. Wein had heard reports that things had calmed down during winter, but the conflict could start to stir again at any moment.

Pleaaaase don't let us run into any trouble, Wein prayed from the bottom of his heart as the carriage swayed.

That was when he noticed Ninym at his side intensely staring at something.

"Whatcha lookin' at, Ninym?"

"A map. I'm checking our route." Her eyes never left the page. "Based on our information from Hagal, it seems the Remnant Army is based around here. We have to pass through as swiftly and silently as possible—or we'll get spotted. There are three roads that will take us to Cavarin's royal capital, but the central one may be our safest option. The shortest is along a cliff, and there's talk of occasional landslides. In terms of our schedule, it seems— Wein?"

"Sorry, let me see that for a sec." Wein took the map from Ninym's hands, cracked open the window, and leaned outside.

"Hmm…"

The delegation was passing through some hills, the area marked by the barren, undulating terrain. At a quick glance, Wein could see potential hiding spots. Way off into the distance, he could make out a forest. It was still blanketed in snow, and after checking the map on hand, he beckoned Raklum, whose dubious look seemed to question if something had happened.

"Your Highness, is something troubling you?"

"This map shows that forest ahead of us. What do you think?"

"……" Raklum compared the map and terrain—and his expression changed from calm to stern. "…It was impossible to tell from the map alone, but I am suspicious of these surroundings now that we're here."

"Exactly my thoughts. Send a few scouts ahead. Hagal says there are bandits galore—in addition to soldiers from Marden and Cavarin."

"Understood." Raklum quickly relayed the instructions to his subordinates, and three horsemen raced off toward the craggy rock face ahead.

With bated breath, the onlookers observed the delegation from the shadowy hills.

"—You think they noticed?"

"Not yet. But it's only a matter of time."

Their faces were hidden by cloth, and they held swords and spears in hand.

"They have…fifty escorts, huh? Just like we'd heard."

"I bet they could have culled some more people from that guard detail. Damn that useless deadwood."

"What should we do, Captain?"

"We don't have much choice. We'll start ahead of schedule."

Things were set in motion.

"——Wha—?!" Raklum was the first to notice something was off. "Enemies! Troops, ready your weapons!"

The guards quickly responded to his raised voice. Wein was impressed by their swiftness as they readied their swords and spears. But for all that, it didn't negate the advantage of the enemy's surprise attack. On both sides of the road, dozens of assailants appeared, charging into their procession.

"Wein! Get down!" Ninym yanked Wein and pushed him to the carriage floor.

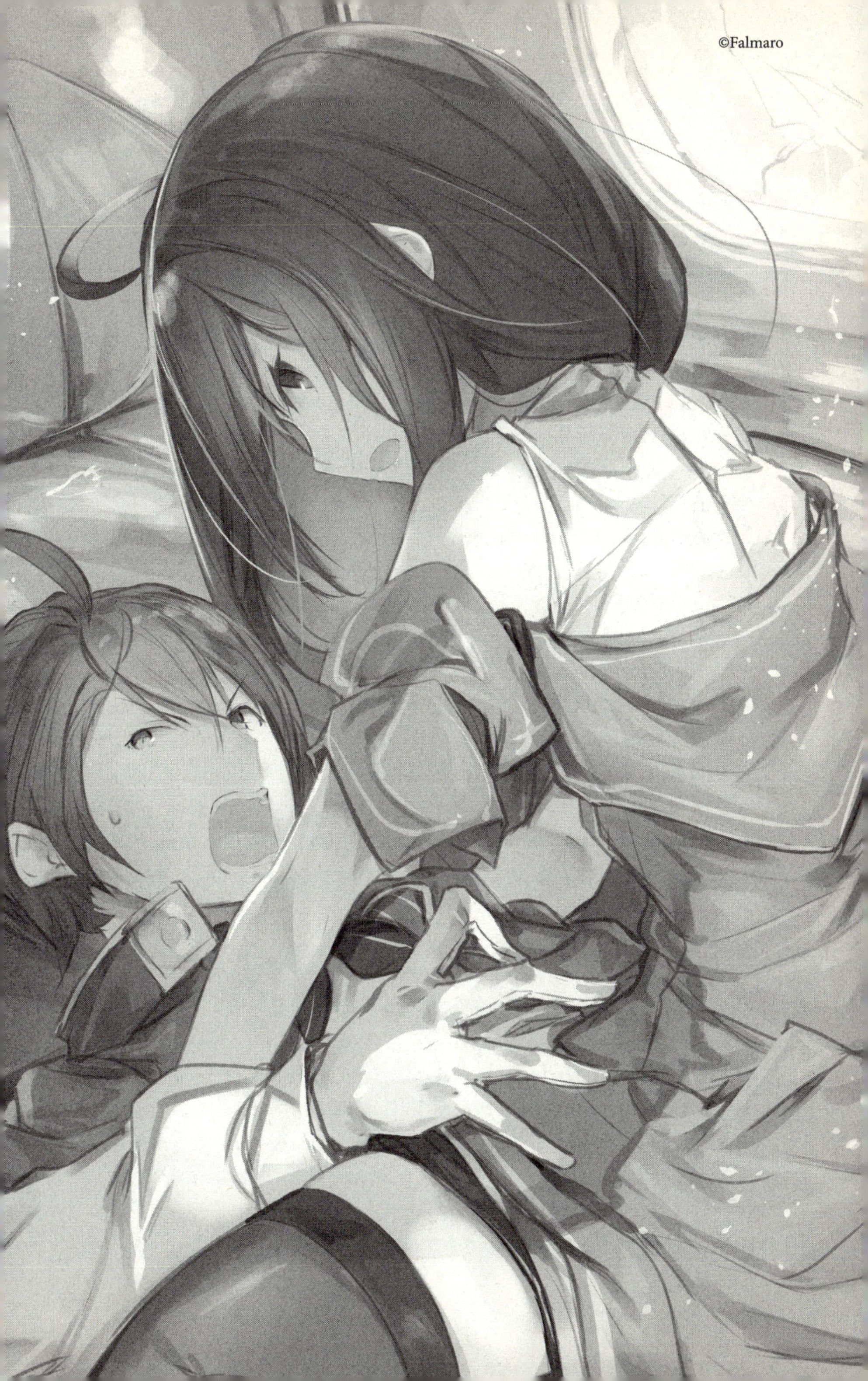

A beat later, one spear shot straight over their heads—then two. Another grazed past the coachman up front as he tumbled over.

"Protect the carriage!" Raklum's voice echoed from outside.

From the fierce bellows and sudden clash of swords, Wein knew the battle had begun.

"Your Highness! Are you all right?!" shouted Raklum.

Inside, Ninym answered as she continued to hold down Wein. "He's alive! What's the situation?!"

"A pincer attack! We're at a disadvantage! The enemy— Get outta my way!"

They heard the whistling of a sword and then a bloodcurdling shriek. Blood sprayed across the passenger window.

"We don't know who the attackers are! Their numbers and skill are about equal to our own! I propose forcing our way through!" Raklum sounded uneasy.

Above Wein, Ninym listened as a shiver went down her spine, realizing the situation was dire.

But Wein's mind was already one step ahead. Which *one is it—?!*

The delegation consisted of about fifty experienced elite soldiers. But their opponent appeared to possess the same numbers and skill. To execute this perfect pincer, it couldn't be the work of average bandits.

So who were they?

Wein already had the answer.

They're soldiers disguised as bandits! They immediately targeted the carriage because they're after me! If I had to guess, there's a good chance that it's either Cavarin or the Remnant Army!

In an instant, Wein had pieced together his theory, which was how he arrived at his earlier question: *Which one?*

There are clues, but it's impossible to be sure. In that case, let's take a bet!

As more thoughts and theories whizzed through his mind, Wein quickly made his decision.

"Raklum!" Wein yelled. "I'm leaving this area up to you! The two of us will hightail it out of here!"

"Understood! Take guards with you!"

"No need! Give these guys all you've got! If you give us too many of your men, they'll crush you here and come after us!"

"But, Your Highness, that means…!"

"It's fine! Ninym, take the driver's seat! But don't move forward! I'm sure they've set a trap!"

Closed in on both sides, it would be hard to turn the carriage back around. To escape, they would have to move forward, but Wein instinctively knew a trap lay ahead.

"Then, which way?!" Ninym shouted back.

Wein yelled his answer.

Finally, Ninym and Raklum realized his goal. Wein pulled out one of the lodged spears and busted open the passenger door as he held it in one hand.

"Listen up, everyone!" he boomed in a voice unmatched by Raklum's.

Friend and foe alike took notice of Wein.

"Wein Salema Arbalest is right here!" he shouted, spear in hand.

Everyone took a moment to consider his words. Meanwhile, Wein looked around him and identified the most likely candidates from their battle positions. Among the possibilities, he caught sight of one who had come to his senses and was issuing orders to those around him.

That must be the commander————!

Wein aimed the spear, hurling it at the authoritative man. The bandit noticed and twisted his body instantly but still failed to dodge in time. The spearhead ripped through his leg.

"Now, Ninym!"

"Right!"

At Wein's command, Ninym drove the carriage ahead. Blowing past both enemies and allies, she tried to race out of this unexpected battlefield. They were not heading southwest—but northwest.

"——After them!" shouted the man with the torn leg.

But the bandits couldn't respond fast enough. After all, chasing after Wein meant turning their backs to the soldiers of Natra, which would leave them vulnerable to further attack. But they couldn't help but feel they were letting the target get away—making them unfocused. The Natran soldiers weren't about to let this chance pass them by. As he left the scene, Wein saw the tide of battle immediately shift in their favor.

Good to see they're stuck in place. But now I've got to deal with—

Wein saw a forest come into view on the path ahead. There, a new group jumped out at them.

I knew it! A cavalry unit... Dammit! This doesn't look good!

There appeared to be four horsemen hidden in the forest. Wein clicked his tongue and looked over his shoulder.

"Ninym, full speed! They're catching up!"

"If I do that in this terrain, we'll break the carriage!"

"It's fine! Just go!"

"For crying out loud." Ninym groaned, speeding up the horses.

But the four horsemen doggedly closed in. Wein looked forward for just a moment. The terrain sloped gently, and the sway of the carriage became less unstable as they approached. Wein threw the other spear that had been lodged in the carriage frame.

It skimmed past the enemy horses and embedded itself in the ground.

"Well, yeah, I guess I knew that wouldn't work— Whoa!"

Seeing the enemy ready their bows to retaliate, Wein ducked his head back into the carriage. Arrows struck seconds later.

"Wein, are you okay?!"

"My wallet isn't, thanks to the repairs this carriage is gonna need!"

"That ship sank a long time ago!"

During this quick banter, they heard a strange noise from below. Before they had a chance to think about it too deeply, the carriage was thrown completely off-balance: The axle snapped, and the wheels went flying.

"Crap…!"

The carriage toppled sideways, and the horses tumbled as they were dragged along with it. Wein held on to the cabin wall, enduring the impacts as best as he could while he was thrown around helplessly.

When the carriage finally came to a halt, he crawled out in a scramble.

"Wein!" Ninym ran over and grabbed his hand. She must have immediately leaped off the coachman's seat to safety. But before either had time to celebrate their good fortune, they saw the cavalrymen closing in on them from behind.

"Wein, I'll buy you—" Before she could say "time," Wein put a finger to Ninym's lips.

"No need for that. Watch."

Arrows rained down on the four pursuing horsemen. Ninym whipped around to find a dozen soldiers on top of a hill.

"That's…"

"You got it."

The horsemen fell in moments. As they watched the cavalry get mopped up, several soldiers on horseback came from the top of the hill and approached Wein.

Ninym stepped in front of Wein with open hostility, but he held her back.

"…Have you two any injuries?"

"As you can see, we're just fine. All thanks to you. We owe you one."

"It is enough that you two are safe… That said, it is obvious that you are of noble bearing. Might I ask your name? What business would you have here?"

Wein nodded. "I am the crown prince of Natra, Wein Salema Arbalest."

The soldiers were all shocked. Wein turned to them with a bright smile.

"I came here to meet the commander of the Liberation Front, Prince Helmut. Show me to him."

"…I see, Wein. You knew those bandits were part of Cavarin's army."

"That's right. To be fair, I couldn't really be certain."

Wein and Ninym spoke in a stony room.

"That forest was to the southwest… In other words, a zone under Cavarin's influence. They were trying to herd us there, which meant it couldn't be the Remnant Army."

"So you intentionally turned the carriage toward the Remnant Army to save us. What a risky move."

"It was the lesser evil. And see? Now we've been welcomed in."

"Welcomed, huh…?" Ninym grumbled as she glanced about the room.

After learning about Wein's identity, the soldiers had hastily consulted with one another. In the end, they decided to oblige his request and take him to Prince Helmut, bringing them to a room of this mountain fortress. Based on its appearance, it was apparent that this was an old fortress, even though it had been repaired.

It was as though they had taken an abandoned stronghold and breathed new life into it.

This current room seemed to be mainly used for storage. The

furnishings were minimal, and there were traces of a rushed cleaning job. They could smell the lingering dust. With soldiers stationed outside the door, they were essentially under house arrest.

Many nobles would have been outraged by this treatment, but Wein remained calm. The Remnant Army was in the middle of an ongoing dispute with Cavarin. They had to be short on accommodations and staff. The crown prince of a neighboring nation kind of just fell into their laps. They didn't have the time or energy to prepare a grand welcome even if they wanted to.

"It's fortunate they were considerate enough to ready a room for us. It means they're not about to cut us down."

"You never know. What if they're discussing ways to behead us as we speak?"

"Then I'll persuade them to stop before the blade falls. I'm more worried about Raklum and the others."

"If the enemy is after you, I doubt they're concerned about annihilating your guards. I'm willing to bet they withdrew."

"No, I'm more worried about whether Raklum went crazy with guilt after fending off the enemy."

"…Let's get in touch as soon as possible."

"Yeah…"

An odd look settled across their faces.

Then a knock came at the door.

"Pardon me."

The door opened, and a man stood before them.

Wein's eyes widened in recognition. "…To think we'd reunite here."

A short, small build. A round figure. Wein knew this person.

"Fate is a funny thing. Isn't it, Sir Jiva?"

"Yes, Prince Regent."

And with that, Jiva bowed deeply.

*   *   *

Around the time Wein had usurped the gold mine, a diplomat had been sent from Marden. That man was known as Jiva. Though this diplomat had failed in his negotiations, his skills as a negotiator had given Wein more than enough reason to groan.

Guided by that very same man, Wein and Ninym now walked through the hallway of the fortress.

"But I have to admit I'm surprised that you joined the Liberation Front."

Wein was careful with his word choice to avoid saying *Remnant Army*.

He went on. "Trust me when I say that I'm glad you're okay more than anything else. I heard through the grapevine that there had been casualties when Marden's royal capital was attacked by Cavarin."

"That means everything to me, Crown Prince. Fortunately... Well, that's not the right word. I was saved only because the soldiers of Cavarin went straight for the palace. I was dismissed from my post after failing to conclude a successful deal, waiting to be punished at my personal residence."

"I see..."

As the perpetrator of Jiva's failure, this was a tricky topic for Wein. He quickly switched to safer waters.

"It seems that Cavarin has allowed most government officials to serve the palace. Couldn't you have done the same?"

"I am Marden born and bred. I will burn before serving those who brutalized my nation and the royal family."

Oh yeah, he's that kind of guy, Wein remembered.

Jiva went on. "I am surprised, too. When I heard that the prince regent of Natra had been attacked by bandits and requested an audience with Prince Helmut, I thought it was a ploy devised by Cavarin."

"That's no shocker. I would have been suspicious, too. I'm glad you were here, Sir Jiva. You know me."

"I am pleased to see that no misunderstandings have arisen between us." Jiva flashed him a shrewd look. "I have great respect for you as a person. But you mustn't forget that I serve the royal family of Marden and Prince Helmut."

"Of course. That's what makes a loyal subject."

"Oh, please, Your Highness… Well then, we're here."

Before them was a conspicuously large door. Jiva rapped his knuckles on it.

"Prince Helmut, I am here with our two visitors."

The door opened with a rusty creak to reveal a room that must have been normally used for war councils. Among the several soldiers awaiting them was one eccentric-looking man.

"…So you're the crown prince of Natra," said a muffled voice.

It was muted for an obvious reason. The speaker wore a full suit of armor indoors.

"I am Helmut, the second prince of the Marden Kingdom."

Which meant Wein was going to have to negotiate with this armored man. Even Wein was thrown by this whole situation.

What the heck is going on…?

Helmut's face was covered with a metal helmet—save for narrow slits for him to see and breathe out of. Even Wein wouldn't be able to discern his character through those openings alone.

"It is an honor to meet you, Prince Helmut."

It didn't matter what was going on. Prince Helmut had just introduced himself, which meant Wein had to return the gesture in kind. Wein bowed.

"I believe you already know that I'm Wein Salema Arbalest, the crown prince of Natra. There are a number of topics I wish to discuss with you, but first, I want to express my thanks. Your Liberation Front saved me from a life-or-death situation. And for that, I am grateful."

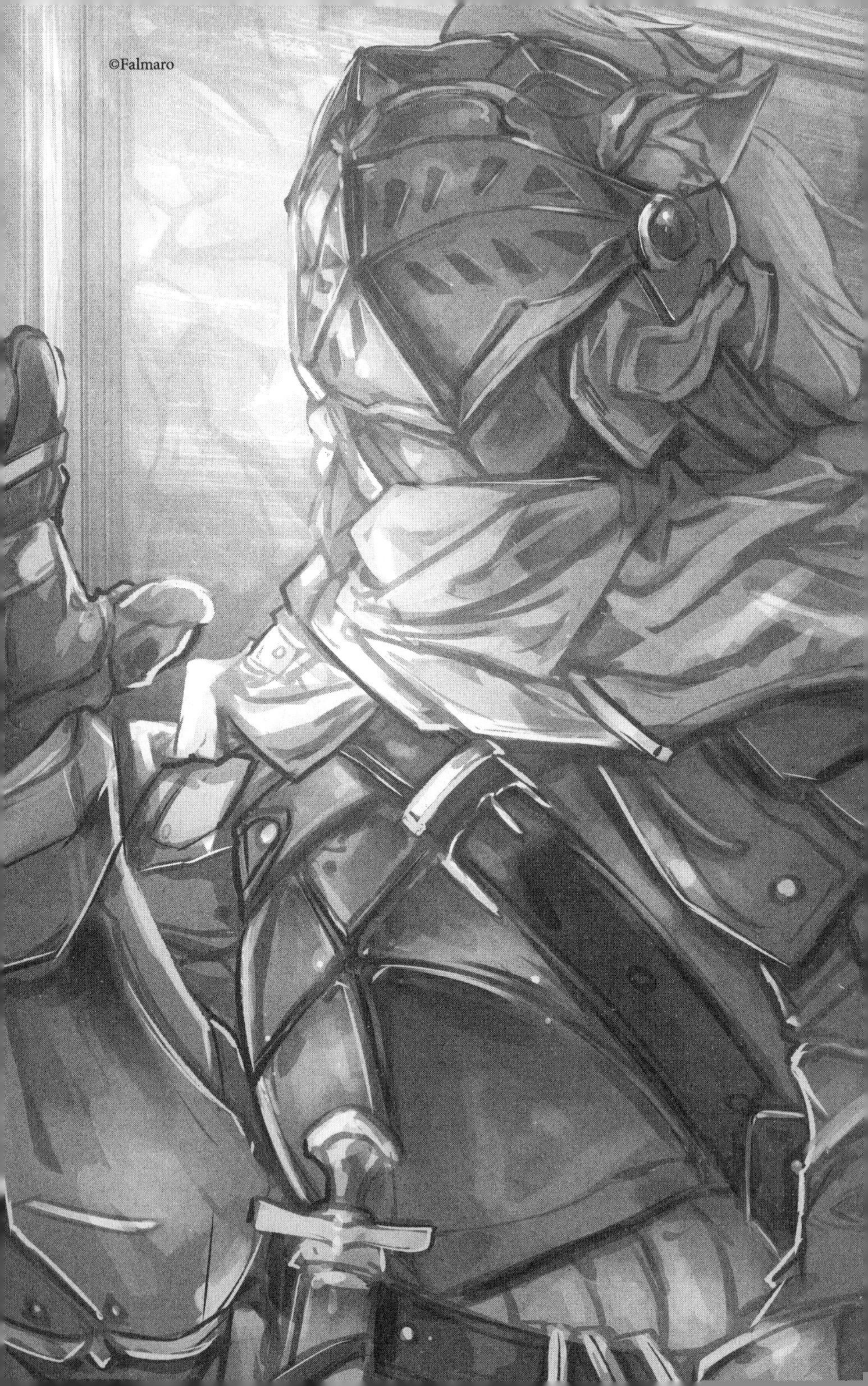
©Falmaro

"Don't mention it. As the crown prince of Marden, it is my duty to suppress bandits. In fact, we should be criticized for our own ineptitude—allowing them to run free and thrive out there."

"Prince Helmut, that is not..." Jiva hurriedly tried to interject, but Helmut silenced him with a single hand.

As Helmut sat down, Wein sat in a chair across the desk.

"So is that all you wanted to say?" Helmut asked.

"There is one more thing... Why do you wear armor indoors?"

"...As the royal capital fell, I was temporarily captured by the Cavarin army. They burned my face." Helmut stroked his helmet with a finger in his gauntlet. "In that moment, I made a vow to God. I was a member of the royal family and allowed the capital to fall. To atone for my sins and fulfill my royal duty to revive Marden, I vowed to never show myself before others until the capital is restored."

"...My, that's certainly something," replied Wein, casting a glance at Ninym standing at attention next to him.

Whaddaya think? he asked with his eyes.

Super-shady, she wordlessly replied.

Got that right.

He wore armor to hide his burn scars and as a reminder to himself and his allies. It checked out logically. But Wein and Ninym couldn't help but feel like he was really playing it up.

Could he be a body double? This probably isn't the right time to press the issue.

Wein and Ninym were completely defenseless, surrounded by armed soliders. They both had concealed weapons, but the chances of them battling their way through the situation was basically a coin toss. If they added a successful escape into the equation, those chances grew even lower.

Guess we'll just roll with it.

It didn't matter to Wein if this was the real Helmut or a double.

The Liberation Front interacted with him as though he were Helmut and obeyed his orders. That was what mattered.

"It appears that I have asked an uncouth question. Forgive me, Prince Helmut."

"Think nothing of it. Why don't we get to the heart of the matter?" Helmut was starting to get more intimidating.

The verbal war between the princes was about to begin. All present held their breath.

"Prince Wein, please tell me why you've come here."

That had to be the meat of the conversation.

Jiva thought as he listened in.

We never received any word that they wished to discuss anything with us… It's obvious they were trying to cross the country in secret. Plus, we have information that an emissary from Cavarin entered Natra's capital…

The Remnant Army realized Natra was trying to join together with Cavarin.

Ninym was having some thoughts of her own.

Regardless of what they know, we can't be honest about our intentions. That will naturally set them against us… From the Remnant Army's point of view, a relationship between Natra and Cavarin would spell out their demise.

The subject was unavoidable, but there would probably be blood if they failed to carefully sidestep it.

How would Wein answer?

Everyone looked on with bated breath.

"I am on my way to attend the Festival of the Spirit in Cavarin's royal capital," he replied.

Chatter broke out around them.

Does this person hesitate at anything—?! Jiva couldn't hold back the shiver that went down his spine.

At this rate… We should probably ready ourselves.

Ninym gently lowered her center of gravity in preparation to move at any time. The only ones who remained still were Wein and Helmut.

Helmut had his face covered.

Wein was flashing a bold smile as he added fuel to the fire. No one else in this situation would have been able to keep such a brave face.

"…Do you understand what you are saying? If you wish to take it back, now is the time, Prince Wein."

"I only speak the truth. What have I said that I should take back?"

"In that case—" Helmut reached for the sword at his side. "There is no other choice but for you to die here."

The air froze over. Helmut wasn't the only one tightly gripping his weapon; the guards stood ready with theirs as well. Ninym and Jiva had adopted nervous looks—but Wein started to chuckle, laughing loudly enough to catch them all off guard.

"…What's so funny?"

"Ah, sorry. That was rude of me. I have one question: What do you think would happen if you killed me here?"

"I'd prevent an alliance between Cavarin and Natra."

"And?" Wein's eyes sparkled terribly. *"Do you honestly think the Liberation Front can beat Cavarin that way?"*

It was the guards who flared up in anger.

"H-how dare you!"

"Are you suggesting we'd lose against *them*?!"

A chorus of shouts started to form, but Helmut only had one thing to say. "Silence."

That was all it took to hush the guards. They obeyed not out of fear but loyalty. Wein admired his leadership.

"…Why would we ever lose?"

"It's simple. Cavarin can mobilize over twenty thousand soldiers. How many do you have in the Liberation Front? Even a generous estimate would put your numbers around two or three thousand."

Natra had investigated the Remnant Army. There was no questioning the count.

Wein went on. "Last year, Cavarin was quiet as they settled into their newly occupied territory and holed up for the coming winter, but this year, there's no denying that they're ready to crush you. Does the Liberation Front have a plan to stop them?"

"......"

"Let's say you killed me. It might buy you some time. But you should only buy time when you know you'll come out stronger by the end of it. As more time passes, things will only get worse for the Liberation Front."

He deliberately didn't say it, but Wein saw the late King Fyshtarre's government missteps as a liability for Helmut.

It wasn't as though Cavarin was particularly good at governing their occupied territories. But foreign occupation still offered the Marden citizens respite from Fyshtarre's mismanagement.

If it were me, I would have aimed to recapture the royal capital before winter rolled in, even if the chances were slim.

Before passions cooled. Before wounds had time to heal. Before the people could get a taste of peace.

They should have screamed about Cavarin's atrocities, incited the people, and fought with all they had.

But that wasn't what happened. Wein wasn't sure why, but as a result, the Remnant Army had missed out on their chance to take back the capital.

"...In other words, you think we're already done for. You think we should just let you go," barked Helmut in anger. His hand reached for the hilt of his sword again, but unlike the earlier threat, he clearly intended to go for the kill.

Wein's smile grew all the more arrogant rather than atoning for his mistakes.

"Far from it. I'd like to offer a more constructive proposal."

"A proposal…?"

"Indeed," Wein prefaced. "Prince Helmut, have you never considered sending people with me to Cavarin?"

Confusion spread. Their reactions went beyond surprise. Seeing his opening, Wein continued.

"My delegation may have been attacked by bandits, but I know it was the work of Cavarin."

"…I do not see how you could come to this conclusion. What reason would Cavarin have to do that?"

"I'm making this proposal because I don't know," Wein admitted. "But I have every intention of going to Cavarin. Depending on the circumstances, making an alliance with the Liberation Front can be very advantageous for me. If that's the case, wouldn't it save us time to have people from the Liberation Front on the inside?"

Wein pressed further.

"The Holy Elites will gather in their royal capital this year. Security will be tight, but as a member of the delegation, you'll be able to enter with no problem. This gives you the opportunity to make contact with them."

"Hmph…"

All the other Western nations had been silent about Cavarin's surprise attack on Marden. Since it was a country ruled by a member of the Holy Elite, denouncing them was tricky, diplomatically speaking. However, what if criticism was leveled at them by another Holy Elite of the same rank? There was no way all of them agreed with Cavarin's methods. If they could somehow show the Holy Elites that there was merit in opposing Cavarin, there was a chance to gain supporters.

…They're frightening, terrifying people.

Listening to the princes' conversation nearby, Jiva couldn't help but feel impressed. As things stood, Wein was in enemy territory—yet he had boldly entered negotiations without showing a trace of fear and now held the rapt attention of everyone present. He had complete control over the conversation.

The plan itself isn't necessarily a bad one. The key is whether these negotiations will lead to an alliance with Natra.

As Wein had pointed out, the Liberation Front was in a tight spot: limited resources, dwindling personnel, and public sentiment that was only growing more distant… Failure wasn't far off. To prevent that, they needed the aid of other nations, but winter had come and gone without any support materializing.

That was where the crown prince of Natra had come in with his sudden proposal. It was true that Wein was doing all the talking, but he was voicing his suspicions of Cavarin and pointing out the possibility of an alliance—even though Marden had nothing to offer.

He doesn't respond to threats or intimidation tactics. Holding him hostage will only make his people angry. That's out of the question. Your Highness should accept his proposal here to deepen ties… Jiva's eyes signaled his armored master.

"I admit your proposal is worth consideration," Helmut started.

"Well, then—"

"*However*," Helmut interrupted, "I have some concerns. I wonder if this is all a lie that you concocted so you can escape. I wonder if I should actually believe you."

Jiva was surprised at first, but then he thought it over. There was a point of compromise. Helmut was bargaining to see if he could get anything more out of this.

"Of all the things to say," Wein replied.

His response was beyond the imagination of everyone in the room.

"*Isn't that exactly why you should go for it?*"

"What are you trying to say…?"

"Listen, Prince Helmut, this all comes down to trust. Trust only has value because there's the potential of betrayal. It could all be a lie.

You could get tricked. But overcoming your fears to trust… That's how to reach someone's heart." Wein grinned. "Prince Helmut, I'll ask again… Are you sure you can't trust me?"

It was a complete one-eighty.

Nothing for Marden to offer? That just wasn't true.

Wein was asking Helmut to show him what he was worth—in return for his help.

Helmut had come to an answer.

"…Very well. I shall believe in you, Prince Wein."

"You'll soon see you've made the right choice, Prince Helmut."

The two shook hands, and the meeting came to a temporary conclusion.

"Looks like we got out of that somehow," Wein muttered, leaning in his chair, back in the other room.

"I was so scared he would draw his sword," Ninym replied, standing next to him. "And? How much of that did you actually mean?"

"Basically, all of it. I think Cavarin is up to something fishy, and I figured there was a possibility of teaming up with the Remnant Army. Well, we won't know how things will play out until we get there."

"…Let's say you ally with the Remnant Army. Do you think you can win against Cavarin?"

"We'll think about that after—*if*—we actually team up."

A knock at the door. "Pardon me, Prince Regent. We contacted your delegation not long ago, and—"

"Your Highness!"

As Jiva opened the door, Raklum pushed him aside. "I'm terribly sorry that I'm late! I am beyond overjoyed to know you are safe!"

"I'm glad to see you're looking well yourself."

It all happened so fast. The Remnant Army must have already known the location of the delegation. But based on Jiva's expression, it would seem he hadn't expected Raklum to barge in.

"I'll save the particulars for later. How are the troops?"

"Right! After we became separated, the bandits withdrew, and we suffered minor casualties. We are now on standby at the arranged campsite. I sent word to General Hagal, and he will soon be dispatching soldiers to scout the area and resupply us," reported Raklum.

Wein nodded in satisfaction. "Your performance was admirable. I have no intention of blaming you for that attack. I'm still counting on you to command the others."

"Understood! I will do everything in my power to ensure this never happens again!"

"You might have already heard, but members of the Liberation Front will be joining our party. As for how many…" Wein glanced at Jiva, who stood behind Raklum.

"We have chosen to send five," Jiva replied. "Besides the one who shall be their representative, all have battle experience."

"Well, you heard the man. Until you arrive at the capital of Cavarin, those four will also be under your command. Is that okay with you, Jiva?"

"Yes, of course." Jiva nodded. "Prince Regent, I have called our representative for introductions. I hope you do not mind."

"Oh yeah. Sure, no problem."

Jiva moved aside as someone appeared from the other side of the doorway.

"It is a pleasure to meet you, Prince Wein. My name is Zeno," called out the representative who was about Wein's age.

The boy had androgynous features. There was an elegance in his movements that one might expect of a representative.

"This is my nephew. Though he is young and inexperienced, he

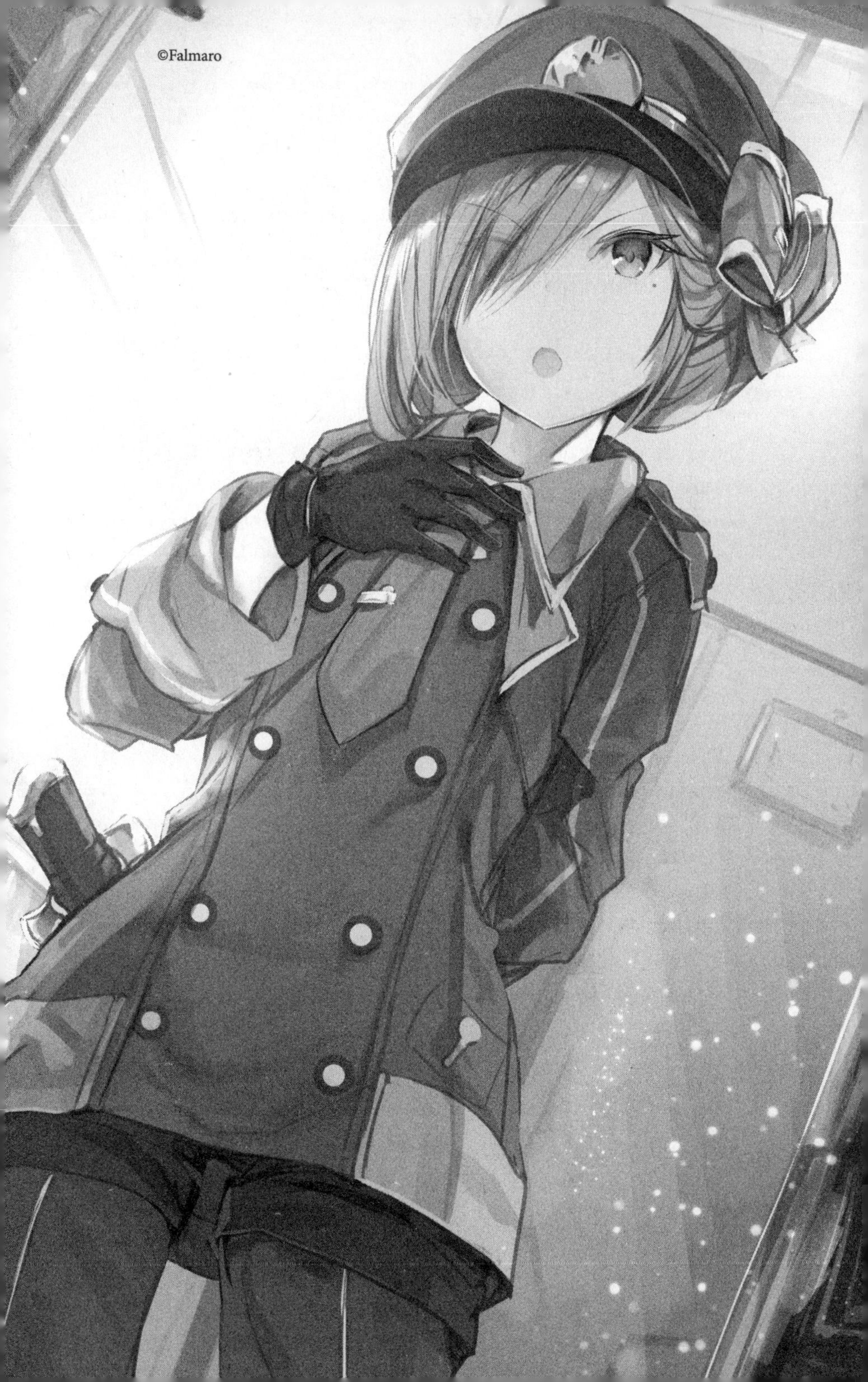

is a master of etiquette. I promise he will not cause trouble for your entourage—" rambled Jiva.

Wein whispered to Ninym, "…This is bad."

"What?"

"This Zeno guy is hotter than me."

"Uh-huh."

"…Did you have to agree right then?!"

"How should I know? Anyway, Wein… This person might be…"

"Yeah?"

Something felt off. Wein took a closer look at Zeno.

Zeno seemed to get more attractive by the second. He was svelte. Even though he carried a sword, he didn't seem tough. In fact, if he donned a dress, he'd definitely be mistaken for a girl—

…*Hey, wait! He* is *a girl!* Wein was close to dribbling spittle.

The clothes and mannerisms did a good job of hiding it, but by looking very, very carefully, he could see that Zeno was unmistakably a girl.

"Um… Sir Jiva."

"Yes?"

"My eyes may be playing tricks on me, but this boy—"

"Prince Regent," Jiva cut him off curtly. "Our Liberation Front is terribly short on people."

"Uh-huh."

"Which leaves us with very few options for skilled diplomats who are unlikely to raise alarm bells when you reach Cavarin."

"Also true."

"And men have the upper hand when meeting the most influential people in the West."

"No objections here."

"In conclusion, Zeno is my nephew."

"R-right on…" Wein looked at Zeno. "Are you okay with that?"

"Of course, Prince Regent. If that is to be my role, I shall accomplish any duty required of me."

With a determined gaze, Zeno nodded. If that was the case, Wein had no more to say.

I don't get the impression that this is just an elaborate trap to keep an eye on me. Plus, it's true that they're short on personnel.

Wein remembered Ninym's earlier question: whether they could actually defeat Cavarin by joining with the Remnant Army.

Wein answered with some uncertainty. "Got it. Well then, let's meet up with our delegation."

And thus, Wein brought along Zeno as the head of the dispatched Remnant Army unit and once again set off for the capital of Cavarin.

Zeno's group joined up with Wein's delegation, and all were on their way, making good progress without running into trouble. They still looked over their shoulders for bandits, but the party started to relax once they passed through the disputed territory and entered the Kingdom of Cavarin proper. They weren't losing focus—or becoming inattentive. It simply wasn't possible to constantly remain on high alert, especially on a long journey. Anyone who tried would collapse midway from exhaustion. Moderation was key.

Not that this changed anything.

The source of these problems came from the members of the Remnant Army—and Zeno in particular.

The road to the capital of Cavarin was long and time-consuming. Meaning they had time to kill. There were miscellaneous matters, of course, like adjusting the speed of their march forward and providing accommodations, but since Ninym and Raklum could handle these issues, it left Wein with too much time on his hands.

If he had been in a carriage, he could have passed the time sleeping. But the carriage had been destroyed in the bandits' attack, and the Remnant Army didn't have any to spare, so he was riding along on a horse, which really wasn't a prime spot for a nap.

Wein had no idea what to do with himself. But Zeno seemed to take advantage of this and approached him.

"Prince Regent, I have a question."

"What could it be today?" Wein answered as they rode side by side. This had become their daily ritual. It usually concerned the politics, ideologies, and culture of Natra.

Guess she's not sick of it yet, he thought with surprise and admiration.

When Zeno had first approached him, Wein was wary, thinking she was using these questions as a pretext to prod about something else. But after a number of conversations, he realized that wasn't the case. It seemed that this girl in disguise was just interested in other nations.

"I'm embarrassed to admit that I'm only familiar with Marden—where I was born and raised. But my narrow understanding of the world does not prepare me to take center stage in national politics, even if we manage to take back the capital. That is why I have never felt more fortunate than I do now with this opportunity to partake of your wisdom, Prince Regent," explained the person in question.

He had no objections to forming a friendship with Zeno, seeing as it was an ideal way to kill time, so he didn't mind answering her endless stream of questions.

"I see…" Zeno said. "As the transit point between East and West, Natra has been influenced by both sides of the continent—not just in food and architecture but language and etiquette, too."

"Our founder was from the West. In the early days, Western influences were more obvious. But in the past hundred years, we've drifted away from the West and gotten closer to our neighbors in the East. That's why you can see Eastern practices in Natra now."

"…Prince Regent, don't those changes concern you?"

Wein shook his head. "I personally don't have an opinion. Some hate change and want things to always stay the same; others love it and embrace it with open arms. Both positions are valid."

"But aren't there times in politics when you must choose to wave one flag or the other?"

"For me—for a politician—to make these decisive calls, you need a proportionate amount of power. Whether I protect the status quo or upheave the entire system, it means I've got access to more power than before. And I don't see a problem with that."

"Are you saying you'd even welcome combat if it comes down to it?"

"I would. Power lies in passion. And passion is a chance for progress. My greatest fear would be for the torch—for our culture—to quietly die out without any promise to preserve or change it."

"I see…" She seemed to be hung up on something, pondering it with concern.

Raklum rode up to Wein. "Your Highness, forgive me for interrupting. I have a few matters I wish to confirm."

"Understood. Zeno, we'll have to stop here for today."

"Yes. I'm grateful for your kindness, Prince Regent." Zeno bowed and slowed her horse's pace, moving to the back of the delegation.

As Wein spoke with his subordinate, Zeno's eyes bore into his back.

A voice called out beside her. "Oh, did your talk with the prince finish early today?"

It was a black-haired girl on horseback—Ninym.

"Ah, Lady Ninym. Are you free, too?"

"Yes. My only task was to check on our luggage."

Ninym and Zeno. A Flahm in disguise and a girl going incognito. While both had their circumstances, they were friendly with each other—since they were around the same age and some of the only women in the delegation. Upon noticing Wein bored out of his mind, Ninym had been the one to encourage Zeno to be his conversation partner.

"I had heard the rumors, but I'm still in awe of the prince's sharp opinions. From our discussions alone, I can feel my entire worldview shifting." Zeno was unable to hide her admiration.

"It is what makes the crown prince the pride of his subjects."

Ninym nodded in satisfaction. "More than that, Master Zeno, I believe I told you that formal titles are not necessary with me."

"I believe I've said the same."

"Though you may be in disguise, you are the representative of the Liberation Front. Given my rank, I could never."

"But shouldn't I be treated the same as everyone else? I am in a disguise after all. And for all your talk of rank, you mustn't forget that you're the prince regent's aide, Lady Ninym."

"Hmm…" Ninym thought for a moment. "…Even if my position doesn't officially exist?"

Zeno cocked her head. "I understand what you are trying to say, but…unless you change your way of speaking, Lady Ninym, I have no intention of switching anything."

"…You give me no choice." Ninym sighed and gave a small cough. "I guess we can both change, Zeno."

"No complaints here, Ninym."

They were aware they were from different countries with very different goals. But that didn't stop the two girls from sharing a small smile.

"By the way, Ninym, what did you mean your position doesn't exist?"

"It's simple. In Natra, the official position of aide hasn't been publicly established."

Huh? Zeno scrunched up her face.

Ninym faced her as she continued. "As you know, Natra is a nation of immigrants. To prevent the loyalty to the already small royal family from decentralizing, official positions that can act on behalf of the king—including aide and prime minister—have not been put in place."

In short, Ninym was treated as an aide and referred to as one, but on all official accounts, she was no more than a private secretary personally under Wein.

That wasn't the only reason an official position hadn't been established.

"...For generations, Flahm have served as the royal family's aides, right?"

"Yes, that's right," Ninym confirmed.

Zeno nodded in understanding. "I see now. If an official position was created, it might turn into a tug-of-war between them and a non-Flahm over this post. That's why it's kept as a matter of personal employment."

"Bull's-eye."

Being an aide was a job that could bring one into immediate contact with the royal family. It wasn't uncommon for outsiders to try to worm themselves in. In fact, Ninym had, on occasion, found gifts sent to her home. And Ninym was a Flahm. If someone from a privileged race was officially given this position, they would have amassed a fortune from the title alone.

Ninym went on. "Plus, Flahm are a low class who need the royal family's protection. But if we get too friendly with the royals, people will perceive us as dangerous—because we're Flahm—and try to drive us out. That's why we're given no rank or title."

"...I'm constantly surprised by cultures in foreign nations. I find them unique. I've been so secluded in Marden that I haven't had the chance to learn much about them." Zeno sighed in wonder.

Ninym shrugged. "If we're talking about unique, I'd say you're no less."

"If you mean my appearance, that doesn't count."

Zeno fumbled with her clothes, touching her lapel. She had acted determined in front of Wein, but it seemed she had her own personal opinions on her appearance.

Ninym gave her a wry smile. "That's not it. I mean the way you're acting with a Flahm like me."

"Ah, I heard about you from Jiva…my uncle. I was surprised because your hair's black, but it makes sense if you dyed it."

"But you're a follower of Levetia, aren't you?"

"There are people whose homes have been destroyed by their Holy Elites," Zeno answered ominously.

This time it was Ninym who flashed her a look of understanding. "'The enemy of my enemy is my friend'?"

"Things would be simpler if we could categorize feelings into easy terms… But at any rate, I have no intention of looking down on you for being Flahm."

"I'm glad to hear it." This came from the bottom of Ninym's heart.

Right on the heels of their conversation, a commotion erupted at the front of the delegation. The girls readied themselves for an enemy attack, but it was something else. The foremost group had just crested a small hill and come to a halt.

Wein waved to them from the center. "Ninym! Come look at this!"

She urged her horse onward in response, and Zeno followed behind as if lured in.

As they reached the top of the hill, their eyes widened.

"That's…"

Inside a thick castle wall was a magnificent city neatly lined with colorful buildings.

The royal capital of Cavarin, Torystoria, stood before them.

"I've never seen it before. It's beautiful," remarked Wein.

Through his short comment, he spoke for everyone present.

"This is the domain of the Holy Elites… The Festival of the Spirit is going to be huge this year," Ninym added.

"It would be nice if we had some downtime to enjoy the festival." With a wry smile, Wein turned to the delegation. "Well, we're almost there. Let's go."

They all nodded and raced toward the capital.

"I have been awaiting you, Prince Regent," said Holonyeh, the diplomat who visited Natra. He greeted them at the city's entrance. "We have prepared a guesthouse. Please, right this way."

Guided by Holonyeh, Wein and the others stepped into the royal capital.

"This is…"

"Oh my…"

The capital was surely a spectacle to behold from the outside, and the interior did not disappoint either, making them all sigh in wonder. The buildings stood tall in neat, little rows, and the streets were immaculate. Most notable was how the city was full of life and movement. The Festival of the Spirit would last a few days, and their party had arrived the day just before it all began. Scores of people had gathered together to take part, and every face seemed to be brimming with excitement.

"It's my first time seeing it, but this really is something." Wein took in the city sights as he swayed on horseback. They were no doubt in Holy Elite territory.

Ninym rode up beside him and secretly whispered her admonition. "If you ogle too much, they'll think you're a country bumpkin."

"But I am a hick. All the way from the remote land of Natra."

"You still have to try to keep up appearances. You're already on a horse because our carriage broke."

"Oh right. Nobles in the West usually ride in those."

A carriage to the side passed them by. From what they could tell at a glance, the passenger was clearly a military man.

"Zeno had brought it up, too, but I guess it's no joke."

"Maybe we should have asked General Hagal to have a new one sent over…"

"There was no time, so we didn't have a choice. That aside, where is Zeno?"

"At the very back so as to not stick out."

To the Remnant Army, this was enemy territory. Their contingent must have fallen back to avoid the worst-case scenario—their identities coming to light. Wein could understand where they were coming from.

"Prince Regent, your guesthouse lies over that way." Holonyeh pointed out what seemed like a brand-new building. In fact, it was *new*-new.

In fact, on closer inspection, it was clear that the structure couldn't have been finished for more than a few days. They had used the Gathering of the Chosen as an excuse to do some urban development.

Must be nice to have all that money.

The royal capital of Natra, Codebell, was considered a historical site—which was a nice way of saying its buildings were old and decrepit. Wein had wanted to fix them up, but his empty pockets prevented him from executing any renovation plans.

As Wein sat there jealously admiring the greener grass on the other side, Raklum stepped forward. "My apologies, Lord Holonyeh, but that building appears too small to accompany everyone in our party."

"I'm terribly sorry. We have many other guests of honor, so we could not prepare more suitable accommodations. We have reserved lodgings at other inns, so I must ask that the other members of your party please stay there…"

In other words, the fancy guesthouses were taken up by the Holy Elites.

Raklum's face couldn't help but twist in displeasure at having his master slighted, but Wein held him back with a hand.

"I don't mind. That aside, Lord Holonyeh, could we can get an audience with King Ordalasse?"

"Yes, tomorrow as scheduled."

"Well then, let's all rest up for today. Raklum will give the delegation members their assignments and stations. Ninym, take care of unloading our luggage. Once that's done, we'll get ready for tomorrow."

""Understood.""

After giving orders to his two loyal retainers, Wein entered the guesthouse.

"—All right."

That evening, the four of them—Wein, Ninym, Raklum, and Zeno—met in a room of the guesthouse.

"I'm obviously going to meet with King Ordalasse tomorrow. I'll bring a number of guards with you at the head, Raklum. I'll let you choose who else is coming."

"Understood!" Raklum bowed in Wein's periphery.

Wein turned to Ninym. "I'd like you to gather information, specifically anything about the king's skill and ideologies, his reputation among his subjects, and his relationship with his officials. Also, get an idea of where the Holy Elites are staying and the city's geography. Take as many delegation members as you need."

"Understood."

As for his meeting with King Ordalasse, Wein saw a high probability of either negotiation or war. He would have liked to bring both Raklum and Ninym—except she was a Flahm. It would create unnecessary trouble if her identity was found out, so he'd given her this assignment instead.

"And Zeno… What about you? If you promise to leave your sword, I don't mind taking you along with me."

Zeno didn't respond. She seemed to be pondering something as she stared blankly into space, but she gasped as their three gazes called her back.

"P-pardon me… By Your Highness's leave, I wonder if I might perhaps join the others in gathering information."

"I see. Feel free to join Ninym. All right, then. Meeting adjourned, everyone."

The three of them bowed, and Zeno and Raklum excused themselves from the room. Only Ninym was left when Wein spoke.

"Ninym, keep an eye on Zeno."

"Yes, that's a good idea. Be careful tomorrow, Wein."

"Hey, if push comes to shove, I'll take Ordalasse as hostage and make my escape."

He had meant it as a joke, but knowing he could do it made Ninym's lips form a tight smile.

The first day of the Festival of the Spirit. The city had come to life.

Jostling crowds. Madness everywhere. Lines for crowded booths and traveling performers displaying their skills in the streets. Colorful petals aflutter. It felt as if spring had arrived.

"Makes you excited just looking at it all," Wein involuntarily murmured as he watched from inside the carriage that came to pick him up.

"I agree. It seems there will also be a band and parade in the early afternoon," Raklum replied, sitting in the carriage as his guard.

"A parade, huh? I definitely wanna check that out."

"In that case, we must see to it that your meeting concludes without incident… Your Highness, depending on how things transpire, be prepared to escape at any moment."

"I know. I'll be on guard."

As they chatted, they arrived at an impressive castle that outshone even the best in the city. As the residential castle of a Holy Elite, its architectural design was heavy with religious iconography, unlike those more often used as bases during war. The inside was unsurprisingly meticulous, and as they took a step inside the main hall, they came across large murals, stretching from wall to ceiling. It was impressive—and overwhelming.

"This…is a marvel."

Raklum had been a commoner when he was appointed by Wein, so he didn't have much of an artist's eye. But even then, the sight of it made him give an involuntary gasp of wonder.

"Levetia preaching to followers… Siblings aiding the poor… The angels discovering Saint Loran… They're all scenes from Levetia's teachings," Wein noted.

"That is impressive, Your Highness. I can appreciate the art, but I'm afraid I am unsure of the details," replied Raklum.

"I'm used to studying this sort of thing. You should take a look at Levetia's holy book when you have the time. If we're going to strengthen ties with the West, you'll get the chance to put that knowledge to work."

"Understood."

Guided by an official who came to receive them, Wein and the others continued through the castle.

Man, this is wild. Starting with those murals, the halls they passed through were lined from corner to corner with luxury. It was a far cry from the dilapidated palace of Natra, and it made Wein hate Ordalasse before he'd even met him—

Just then, several officials appeared from the other end of the hallway.

He assumed they were just passing by, but one elderly man at the front stopped and locked eyes with Wein.

"…Are you Natra's special envoy?"

From his attitude, he must have been a military officer or someone with significant experience on the battlefield. It seemed he didn't have a liking for Wein, snorting as he stared at the young prince.

"How kind of you to come all this way from Natra. I'm sure these sights are unfamiliar to country bumpkins. Enjoy them to your hearts' content."

The face of the official guiding them paled, and the man said nothing more as he left with his attendants.

"I-I'm terribly sorry, Your Highness! F-for you to be treated with such disrespect...!"

He must have thought his own head was about to go flying, bowing down to Wein in a panic. Wein watched him from his periphery as he stared at the back of the man who had just left.

"...And who did I just have the pleasure of meeting?"

"Levert, a general who has served our army for many years..."

"A general, huh...?" murmured Wein before whispering to Raklum beside him. "Calm down. This was nothing."

"Right..."

Raklum had reached for his sword. The veins on his hand pulsed as he clutched the hilt with enough force for his bones to creak.

"Look at the man to the right of that Levert guy," Wein said under his breath.

Raklum followed orders, zeroing in on one of the general's attendants. He realized that though the man was dressed innocently enough, he walked with a slight limp.

"The leader of the guys who attacked us on the way here suffered an injury to his leg... On the same side as that attendant."

"...You can't mean..."

"It's still up in the air. Just don't forget this detail."

"Understood."

After wrapping up their private conversation, Wein urged their guide on, setting off down the hallway once again.

Before long, they arrived at a large door.

"This is the audience hall. Just a moment, please..."

The official slipped through the door while Wein and the others waited outside. A picture on a nearby wall caught their attention.

"…This one feels…different from the rest," assessed Raklum.

Wein nodded. "The merchant and the scales. Illustrates how a money-obsessed merchant had their worldly virtues put on a scale in the afterlife and then fell to hell. However… Hmm."

"Is something bothering you?"

"It's grimmer than the work in the main hall. But the subject matter is common enough. I think the most important detail is that it's been hung in a very public spot."

"Meaning…?"

Just as Wein was about to answer, the official appeared from the doorway. "We are ready for you. This way, please."

The moment of truth. Wein exchanged a look with Raklum and passed through the door, vigilant of his surroundings.

In the audience hall awaited guards; vassals; and a man on the throne, who was dressed in a carefully embroidered robe and wore a brilliant crown. But his clothing didn't outshine his royal bearing, and his features bore the weight of upholding the nation for many years. He was the king of Cavarin and one of the Holy Elite, Ordalasse.

That must be…

Wein slowly inched toward the throne. He could feel the intense suspicion suffusing the room the entire way.

Guess I'm not welcome here.

But he had anticipated this response. In fact, he was used to this sort of thing by now. His main concern was Ordalasse—because Wein couldn't feel any animosity from him at all.

With this dissonance in mind, Wein stopped ten steps from the throne and bowed.

"It is my pleasure to make your acquaintance, King Ordalasse. I am the crown prince of Natra, Wein Salema Arbalest. You have my deepest gratitude for inviting us to your nation—"

Wein had been busy performing his flawless introduction when Ordalasse suddenly stood. He briskly approached Wein—and took his hand without hesitation.

"I'm Ordalasse, the king of Cavarin. Thank you for making the long journey here. I welcome your visit, Prince Wein."

"What? Um. Sure…"

Even Wein was dumbfounded. It was just not normal for a king to walk up to a visiting dignitary in front of everyone and take their hand. He started to wonder if this was Ordalasse's usual habit, but based on the looks of the vassals, that didn't seem to be the case.

"I'd been thinking for a while that I wanted to chat with you. I'm thankful for this opportunity. That said," Ordalasse went on, "we can't have a meaningful conversation here. Why don't we go elsewhere? I want to introduce you to a select few. Let's get going."

Ordalasse hadn't even waited to finish his own sentence before he started to walk off. The attending vassals locked eyes with one another and hurriedly followed him. Wein and Raklum eyed each other, too.

"…What shall we do?"

"…Well, I guess we've got no choice but to go."

Finding Ordalasse hard to read, Wein hurried after the king.

Just as Wein had reached the throne room, Zeno was alone in the shadows of a back alley, holding her breath. Before her was a large mansion with guards patrolling the perimeter. She peered at the aristocratic home.

This was a block running through a residential area housing many of the city's nobles. It was isolated from the general public, and the clamor of the festival didn't reach this part of town.

Zeno was staring at a carriage stopped in front of the residence. From within, a withered tree of a human emerged—Holonyeh.

Zeno's eyes shot open the moment she saw him, and she went for the sword at her side. As she took on the form of a wild animal seeing its chance, she bent her knees and steadied her breath. Holonyeh's back turned toward Zeno, and—

"Don't move."

Without a single footstep to warn her, Zeno found a knife at her throat. Before she had time to realize it, Ninym stood behind Zeno, whose eyes were wide with shock.

"I'd like to prevent any dead bodies if I can help it."

"…Ninym."

"If you plan on obeying my orders, then put down your sword."

Zeno ground her teeth. In the span of their short conversation, Holonyeh was already entering the large manor. She obviously wouldn't have time to run up behind him. The grip on her sword loosened.

"I thought you might be up to something, but I never imagined it would be attempting to assassinate a high-profile man in broad daylight."

Ninym withdrew the knife at her neck, and Zeno glared at her.

"Don't get in my…"

"In your way? You can bet I will."

Zeno had joined Wein's delegation, and he was of a higher rank than her. It didn't matter if her attack had been a failure or a success: His position would be in jeopardy if her actions raised any suspicion. And Ninym obviously couldn't turn a blind eye to this danger.

Though there's a chance she was aiming for exactly that…

Zeno flashed her a resentful look. Ninym could guess at the reason to some extent, but it didn't seem to simply be part of a plan to prevent the forming of an alliance between Natra and Cavarin.

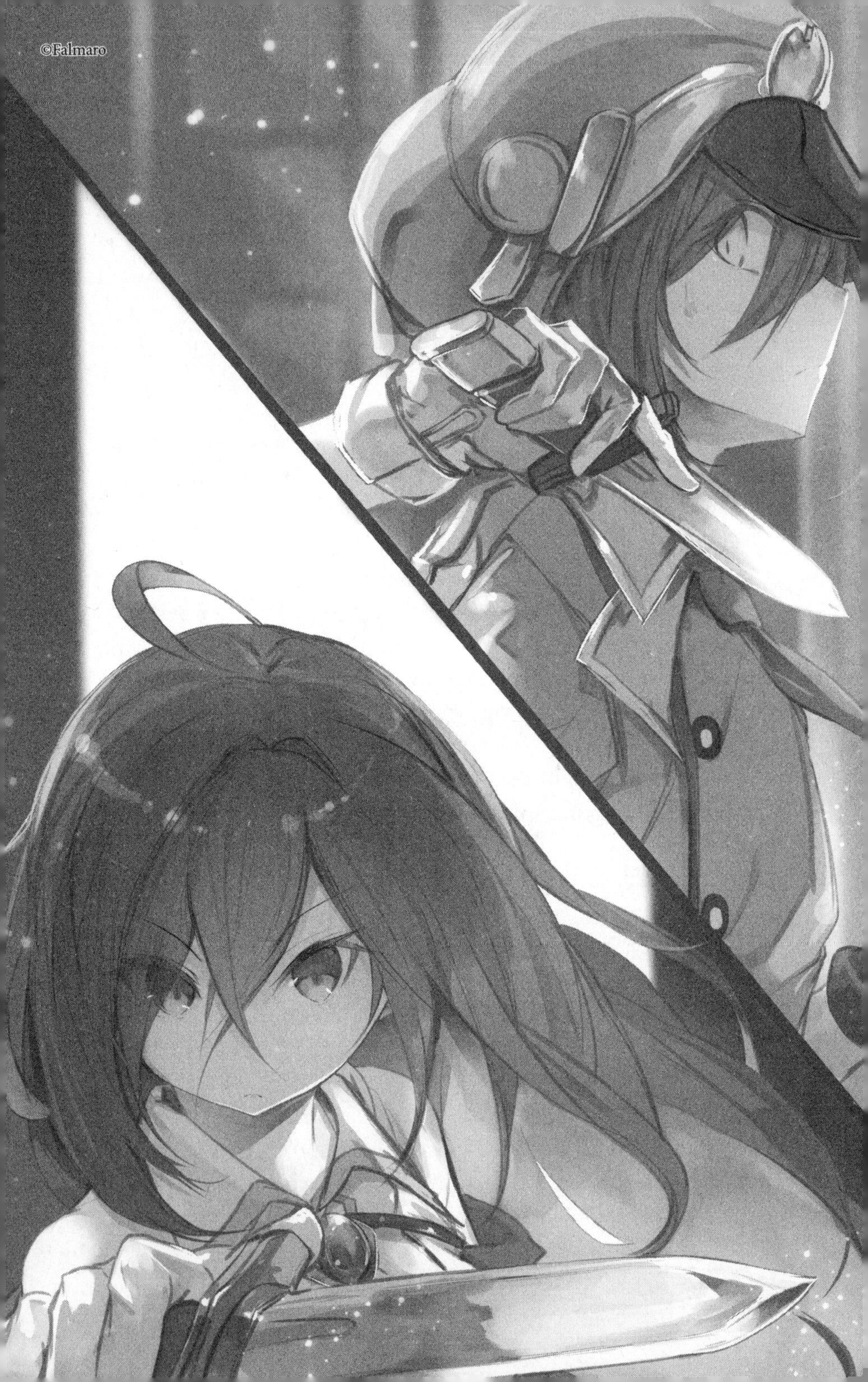
©Falmaro

"In any case, we'd better move. It'll be a problem if someone spots us."

Though Zeno had been ready to go through with her revolt, she silently acquiesced to Ninym's orders and slunk away.

Ninym was heading away from the block of mansions to a place where average citizens could roam. They could start to hear the festival again. Ninym opened the door to a small building and walked in.

"...Where are we?"

"One of the safe houses for spies that we've set up in this city."

Ninym sat down in a nearby chair. At her prompting, Zeno took a seat, too.

"...Are you sure you want to show me this?"

"It's not ideal. But I thought you might need a place to calm down."

"......" Zeno sat in the chair for some time and looked down at her hands. Ninym noticed they were shaking but kept silent.

"...When Cavarin had..." Zeno finally spoke up. "When the news came that Cavarin had broken past our borders to attack, the palace was in an uproar. We had run out of soldiers after the battle with Natra. Of course we were panicking."

"......"

"But the remaining soldiers had gathered together, trying to hold out until the main force at the gold mine could return. And they should have succeeded." Zeno's fist audibly creaked as she squeezed it tight.

"If only that man Holonyeh hadn't betrayed us and opened the castle gate...!"

Oh, I get it now, Ninym thought.

While it was true that Cavarin had launched a surprise attack, the capital of Marden had fallen too quickly. It was because a vassal had secretly betrayed them. She could understand Zeno's hatred toward Holonyeh—and why he had been appointed to his current position by Cavarin.

"If it hadn't been for that sellout, Father wouldn't have…!" Zeno trailed off bitterly.

"What happened to your family during the attack on the capital?" Ninym asked before thinking.

Zeno gasped. "Ah… Th-that's right. They got caught up in the fighting, and…"

Hmm? Ninym thought this was an odd response, but she couldn't pry if she wanted to get closer to Zeno. This was an opportunity to build trust. Ninym changed strategies.

"I understand your situation. But I cannot overlook your attempt to assassinate Holonyeh. In my humble opinion, you ought to get in contact with the Holy Elites in each country to aid your homeland—instead of attempting an assassination."

"That's impossible. I'm only a delegation member. How can I possibly do that?"

"I don't think Prince Wein was summoned to the festival at the same time as the Holy Elites on accident."

"…Do you think I have a chance?"

"At the very least, more of a chance than when you're out there stirring up trouble."

Deep in thought, Zeno closed her eyes for a moment before sighing in lamentation. "…I understand. There are other things to investigate, so I'll take the back seat for now."

"That would really help me out."

For the time being, it seemed Zeno wouldn't be running wild. But Ninym could never be too careful.

"Still… A sellout, huh?" Ninym murmured.

Zeno tilted her head to the side. "What about it?"

"Nothing, I was just wondering what Wein would think if

he heard," Ninym said with a wry smile. Zeno's confusion only deepened.

Things have gotten reeeeeeally weird.

Wein was walking down the castle corridor with his attendants. Ordalasse strode beside him, explaining the paintings and sculpture they passed. Wein expressed his interest at the right intervals to observe proper etiquette as he sunk into private thought.

This welcoming attitude is consistent with his official letter. He must actually want to bolster friendly relations with Natra.

Still, it felt like he was being a bit *too* hospitable. In any case, Wein would keep that in the back of his mind for the moment. He ought to be thinking about his next steps.

But things aren't really adding up if Ordalasse sincerely wants to strike up a friendship. I'll have to ask him what that mid-journey attack was all about.

The idea that the attack was perpetrated by Cavarin soldiers was nothing more than Wein's theory. There was a possibility that they had been normal bandits—with no relation to Cavarin. But would that really be the case?

Hmm… He only had bits and pieces of the entire story. He was grasping at straws, coming up empty every time. He just didn't have enough information.

"Prince Wein," a voice called out, tearing Wein away from his thoughts. The prince looked at Ordalasse.

The king spoke with a solemn expression. "I'm sure you've already noticed with your discerning nature that there's a reason I invited you here now."

"A reason? Whatever could it be?"

"It's nothing to worry about. I'm sure you'll find it to be good news."

Ordalasse paused. Before them was a single door.

"King Ordalasse, will you be introducing me to someone here?"

"Indeed."

Wein could take a stab at the identity of said person. In fact, it was safe to say he was absolutely certain.

It's gotta be one of the seven Holy Elites.

Ordalasse had intentionally summoned Wein right as the Holy Elites were coming together. If the king was trying to introduce Wein to someone, it was hard to imagine anyone else. A Holy Elite close to Ordalasse was no doubt waiting in that room.

And from the way Ordalasse is talking, it's safe to assume he's hoping we'll have a pleasant conversation. Will this go according to my expectations? Is their aim to team up with Natra and strengthen their faction?

It was possible they were after the gold mine. Rather than prioritizing their own nations' factions, it was easier to work on a united front as the Holy Elites. They could then efficiently assess the situation and decide whether to strengthen relations—or something along those lines.

Okay, I'll bite. However…

He had no idea if there would be one Holy Elite or two, but there was no mistaking they were about to put him to the test.

If they think they can get me that easy, they're in for a huge wake-up call. I'll outsmart them all.

The door opened before Wein, who was eager to get started. Wein and Ordalasse entered the room, where they were waiting for the pair with guards.

They numbered one—two—three—four—five—six.

…Hmm?

Huh. That was kind of a lot.

Including the Holy King, there were seven Holy Elites.

And there were currently seven people in the room including Ordalasse.

Funny how those numbers matched.

Hey… Hey, wait a sec…

"Allow me to introduce you, Prince Wein."

Wein's cheek was now twitching.

Ordalasse faced him and spoke plainly. "These are the leaders who support the Teachings of Levetia—the Holy Elites who have gathered in Cavarin for the Gathering of the Chosen."

HOLD UUUUUP! Wein's eyes almost popped out of his head. *You have to be joking! Are you an idiot?! What are you thinking?! I can't believe you'd drag me here without any warning!*

With all the Holy Elites here, this could only be the Gathering of the Chosen: the most important international conference on the Western continent. Every single person present held tremendous influence. As a prince from a tiny northern nation who got dragged in without any warning, Wein couldn't help his reaction. He thought *someone* would be there but never imagined *all* of them.

"…What's the meaning of this, Ordalasse?"

"Just when we thought you'd never get here… You bring us *Prince Wein* of all people?!"

You mean they're just as surprised?!

When the group of six grumbled with skepticism, Wein finally understood this was all Ordalasse's doing.

Wein trembled with irritation. Would Ordalasse really outwit them all and set this casual introduction up?

Nope. *Not a chance.*

Wein frantically ran through ways to take hold of the situation, but it was too late. The chance to retreat was already long gone.

"I have a single proposal for the Holy Elites gathered here."

In the middle of the uproar sparked by him, Ordalasse made a grand proposal.

"I vouch for Wein Salema Arbalest as a new Holy Elite…!"

———*WHAAAAAAAAT?!*

From Ordalasse's proclamation, the situation was thrown into pure chaos.

Even the madness of the festival began to quell as the sun set.

Ninym could feel this change happening around her. Alone in a room of the guesthouse, she scribbled on a piece of paper.

The contents were a summary of her investigations and the information that she obtained on Cavarin. Aside from her own observations, she had included the information about each block of the city she'd gathered from the delegation members, which was a significant amount in itself. Consolidating all this before Wein's return was a part of Ninym's job—but it would appear that something was bothering her.

The reason was obvious. It had to be because he hadn't returned yet.

There hasn't been news of any disturbance at the castle, though.

Maybe she was overthinking things. But she worried nonetheless. Her dread had started to show in her writing: It hindered her progress to a degree. In fact, she had found herself unconsciously scribbling Wein's name.

Without Wein or Captain Raklum here, I can't leave my post… Agh, what a pain!

Just as she looked up at the heavens in irritation, she heard a commotion outside. Ninym flew out of the room, racing through the corridors until she arrived at the hall entrance and found Wein had returned with his entourage.

"Oh, Ninym. Thanks for coming to meet me."

He was alive. He didn't seem hurt, either. As his servant, Ninym bowed to him, reassured.

"—Welcome back, Prince Wein. I am relieved to see you have returned safely."

"Yeah, somehow. But things didn't go quite as planned."

"What do you mean?"

"Something kind of... No... Something *way* beyond my imagination just happened. Anyway, we can talk more about it in private later. Raklum, good work today. I'll leave the rest to you."

"Understood." Raklum started to issue orders to the guards.

As Ninym watched him go from the corner of her eye, she joined Wein down the halls she'd sprinted through, and they entered the room together.

"AAAAAAAAAH! NOOOOOOOOO!" Wein screamed with all he had the moment they were behind closed doors. "To hell with all this! Seriously! Please give me a frigging break!" he whined.

This was a fairly normal reaction for him, but he exhibited less restraint than usual.

"What in the world happened?" Ninym asked.

Wein answered with no attempt to hide his disgust. "...King Ordalasse recommended me as a candidate to join the Holy Elites."

"Huh?"

Wein had broken it down simply, but it still took a few seconds for Ninym to digest it.

When she did, she was shocked. "...You're kidding, right?"

"Nope, I'm serious. A hundred percent. No joke..." Wein answered, throwing himself on the sofa. His haggard appearance seemed to prove the gravity of the situation.

"...I have a bunch of questions for you, but let's start with the fact that there are a number of requirements to become a Holy Elite."

First, you must have experience as a priest.

Second, you must be approved by a majority of the current Holy Elites.

Third, you must offer a satisfactory contribution to be appointed as a Holy Elite.

Finally, you must carry the blood of either the founder of Levetia or one of the lead disciples.

If you didn't meet these requirements, you couldn't become a Holy Elite. No exceptions.

"You could fulfill those in time, Wein, but—"

"Well, to be honest, I already have."

To start, his lineage wasn't an issue. There was hardly a Holy Elite who could match the pedigree of the royal family of Natra. As for priestly experience, while it was only in name, Wein actually did serve Levetia.

When it came down to spreading religion, it made a big difference to have an influential supporter backing it up. This wasn't just limited to the Teachings of Levetia. In Natra—a nation of immigrants, a melting pot of belief systems—it was particularly important to have a strong backer to push Levetia and make sure it wouldn't lose to the competition.

Most members of the royal family of Natra had been serving as Levetian priests since the very beginning. This, of course, could be attributed to their connections in the West dating back to when the country was first founded. However, the tendency in recent years to lean more toward the East was influencing their political balance.

Ninym understood that much, except for one thing...

"There's no way you've contributed enough. You haven't donated a huge sum, built a temple, or anything along those lines."

After all, this was Natra—a nation that was dirt-poor. There was no way they could make any kind of offering that stood out. Plus, if they expressed their outward support toward one religion, it was very likely to cause issues with others in the kingdom.

"That's what I thought, but Ordalasse hammered out an elaborate back door."

"What is it?"

"The war between Natra and Marden was a joint holy crusade with Cavarin to save the believers of Levetia from tyrannical rule in Marden. Which means it counts as a contribution to the Teachings of Levetia... According to him."

Ninym stood in mute shock.

Hearing Wein's sophism was simply a part of her job description. But that was nothing compared to this argument.

"Will... Will that work?" Ninym asked cautiously.

"If we're talking about plausibility, I'd say yes. But it all depends on whether the other Holy Elites will accept me."

The Holy Elites were the most powerful members of Levetia. If they expressed their approval, something could turn white—even if it was black. The remaining problem was the final condition of getting the majority vote. If this condition was met, his contribution to Levetia would be accepted as well.

"...And did they accept you?"

"Not yet. Our meeting was put on hold."

The proposal had been a bolt from the blue for both Wein and the Holy Elites. Of course, everything had become chaos, and they'd been unable to come to a conclusion.

"But to be honest, I was surprised they postponed it. I thought turning me down would be a no-brainer."

"I agree. I would have thought the same thing."

The Gathering of the Chosen and the Festival of the Spirit would be held for the next two days. If they postponed the decision, it meant they were going to lay the groundwork and come up with a game plan.

"...What will you do? Do you really plan on becoming a Holy Elite?"

"There is some benefit," Wein admitted, nodding. "King Ordalasse said that if I can become one, he'll help me get rid of the infamous Circulus Law."

The founder of the religion sought a way to drive away the demons, who caused people strife. Levetia traveled across the continent of Varno, receiving the blessings of the divine for good deeds. This journeyed path had become a pilgrimage for believers.

With advancements in civilization, there were more people than ever making this trip, returning with Eastern culture and ideologies. Fearing Levetia would lose its dominance, the Holy King at the time conspired with legal scholars and proclaimed the Circulus Law. The law, under the pretext of protecting believers from the Eastern barbarians, established a new interpretation of the sacred texts: The believers must only make the pilgrimage on the western half of the continent.

"That certainly would be…momentous," commented Ninym.

When Salema founded the Kingdom of Natra on the northernmost tip of the continent, he had hoped to create a road that allowed pilgrims to pass the border between East and West.

But the pilgrimage was a long journey fraught with danger. If it had been a simple and safe road, there would have been other adherents making this trip. With the Circulus Law, the number of believers coming to Natra had drastically dropped, and the corresponding businesses largely went away. After that, Natra entered an era of bitter winters that lasted a hundred years.

"Right? If I can get rid of the Circulus Law, Natra will see more profit than ever before."

"…I see. As your aide, I completely agree," Ninym said. "However, as a Flahm, the idea of you becoming a Holy Elite makes me uneasy."

The Flahm were discriminated against in Levetia. Though the royal family of Natra had customarily served as priests, they never used religion to oppress the Flahm, which was why the group had accepted this arrangement. But if Wein became a Holy Elite, Ninym was certain there would be more than slight opposition by her people.

"Or maybe"—Ninym hesitated for a moment, then spoke as his aide—"it is all right to cast aside the Flahm if it means you can become a Holy Elite."

"The Flahm have been supporting us for nearly a hundred years. Do you really think I'd do that?"

"You should if it's necessary," Ninym declared.

It was undeniable that Wein held affection for her. But she didn't want him to use her as a reason to ignore the greater picture and prioritize the Flahm against the interests of the kingdom.

"…Well, we can think more about that if it looks like I'll actually be a Holy Elite. Ninym, call Zeno and Raklum. We'll compare notes and decide on our next move."

"Understood."

Ninym followed Wein's orders and left the room. She brought the two back with her a short while later.

"I apologize for the wait, Your Highness."

Ninym was acting courteous now that the two others were present. But her eyes were fixated not on Wein but on Zeno next to her.

It was because the girl's face had grown ghastly pale.

"Is it true that King Ordalasse recommended you as a Holy Elite…?" Zeno asked in a trembling voice.

She must have been thinking about the problems it would pose for the Remnant Army if he accepted this position. If the crown prince of Natra became a Holy Elite, an alliance with Cavarin would be inevitable, and the Remnant Army's chances of winning would essentially drop to zero.

"It's true," he replied calmly as he faced her. "But it's not like it's been totally decided yet."

"…Does that mean you plan to go for the position, Your Highness?"

"I do. There are huge advantages to becoming a Holy Elite, after all."

Carefully watching over Wein from the side, Ninym and Raklum quietly readied themselves should anything happen.

"In that case, we…"

"Hold on. It's too early to come to any conclusions," Wein interjected. "There's usually a catch to these things. We still must find out why King Ordalasse recommended me and the circumstances surrounding it. Depending on the uncovered truth, there's still a chance I'll give up this position."

"……"

"Plus, I intend to set up meetings that will gain me the support of each of the Elites, starting tomorrow—regardless of King Ordalasse's intentions. This is a rare opportunity, after all. When the time comes, I promise to bring you along if you wish."

Though whether you're successful all depends on you.

As Wein concluded, Zeno agonized for a moment.

"…I understand. I'm grateful for your kindness, Prince Regent."

"All right, then. Well, Ninym, go ahead and explain the results of today's investigation."

"Yes!" Ninym took out the report that she had been writing earlier. "First, King Ordalasse's reputation with the townspeople is decent overall. As a Holy Elite, he's one of the most powerful members of Levetia's order and highly respected. However," she continued, "upon investigation, it seems he is estranged from the government officials and feudal lords."

Zeno gave a small nod. "…My information is largely the same. The senior general named Levert, in particular, objects to King Ordalasse's national policies."

Levert. The man from the castle popped in the back of Wein's mind.

"Were you able to find out why?"

Ninym nodded. "It primarily concerns King Ordalasse's policy of jus sanguinis, the right of blood, which states that citizenship depends on one's parents."

"Jus sanguinis? I don't think it's all that unusual."

Whether due to residual animal instinct or not, it was common for people to regard their own child as the best. That was why bloodlines were important—in the past and present, East and West, young and old, men and women.

However, those with power placed a particular importance on blood.

There are multiple reasons for this. For example, many second and third generations of an influential bloodline used their blood as a reason to lay claim to a predecessor's fortune. The opposite was also true: Scorning a bloodline meant kicking aside an identity and legitimacy as the heir.

To someone who was first in line, blood was just as important. Most would oppose a stranger from inheriting and claiming the fortune of a gifted person who had saved up for decades. If there was a conflict over succession, there were times that fortune was squandered.

By adopting a universal value system of bloodlines, the candidates were narrowed down, curbing the risk of a fight over succession.

For example, the Emperor's four children in the East were currently competing for the right to assume the throne. It had been whittled down to only the four of them because of their bloodlines. If everyone thought they could become Emperor, the entire eastern half of the continent would fall into chaos.

"You are right, Your Highness. That said, King Ordalasse seems a *bit*—er, *quite* extreme. He fixates on birth to the point that he's appointed chief vassals who are completely incompetent." Zeno went on.

"And he exercises preferential treatment toward his citizens.

While he is moderate in his policies for free citizens, he is very harsh on discriminated classes, the poor, and slaves. The other day, they renovated the town for the festival—while forcing out the impoverished, who have become sacrifices. From what I heard, it's called the Hunt, used to drive out and kill slaves."

"I see…" Wein nodded. "Back to Levert. Does he control the military?"

"Yes. However, he is the opposite of Ordalasse—*too* devoted to meritocracy, completely scorning bloodlines and authority. He believes in pulling yourself up by your bootstraps to work your way up the ranks. It's hard to imagine why he's popular otherwise." Ninym shrugged and provided supplementary information.

"He allegedly opposed the cease-fire with Natra after the fall of Marden and repeatedly proposed taking back the mine—though this never materialized once they were chased out by the Liberation Front."

It would be great if they could find someone who was ideologically in the middle between Ordalasse and Levert. But reality wasn't very kind.

"That is all the information we have so far. We have the locations of where the Holy Elites are staying and a map of the city. Please review it later."

"Good work," Wein praised. "Well, let's talk about the plan for tomorrow. Three of the Elites agreed to meet with me. You coming along, Zeno?"

"Yes. I am in your care."

"Raklum, gather more information with Ninym tomorrow. Since I'm meeting with the Elites, I don't want to bring anyone who seems like a threat."

"Understood. But I hope guards will accompany you should something happen."

"I know. Choose a few who are less threatening."

Raklum nodded.

"Ninym, look for anything important related to Levert. There's a possibility that either he or someone in his faction attacked us on the road."

"Understood."

"That should be just about it. It looks like tomorrow will be another busy day. Fall back and get some rest."

""Understood."" The three bowed and left the room.

"Well, I wonder how all this will work out…"

With his meeting with the Holy Elites on his mind, Wein continued to think, alone.

The second day of the Festival of the Spirit had arrived.

The festive revelry started and ended on the first day, but the second day offered spectacles by the performers in the plaza of each block. There would even be mock battles on horseback. The spectators were sure to be excited.

Unfortunately, Wein had no time to enjoy any of it.

"I apologize for the wait. Please, right this way."

Guided by a servant, Wein entered the mansion, followed by Zeno and a group of guards. It was more spacious than the one Wein had been allotted and carried a historic air.

Which was just the way it should be. After all, the person staying here was a Holy Elite.

"—I thank you for your invitation, King Gruyere."

Upon arriving in the reception hall, Wein faced the person seated in the center and bowed.

"Welcome, young prince of Natra." The Holy Elite looked at Wein and gave a haughty smile.

*   *   *

Meanwhile, Ninym was following Wein's orders to gather intelligence. Continuing her work from the previous day, she was again skulking around the block of noble mansions. After some investigation, she found that her target—Levert—had a residence there.

"...That's fine and all, but the patrols sure are tight."

She was hiding in the shadows of an alleyway and observing the mansion from a good distance away. Ninym thought about keeping a low profile and digging around for more information, but when she considered even the slight chance of being found out, it just didn't seem realistic.

As she wondered what she should do, she felt a presence close behind her and turned around.

"There you are, Lady Aide."

It was Raklum. Now that he'd been temporarily relieved from his duties as Wein's guard, he appeared to be a completely ordinary fellow.

"How were things over your way?" she asked.

According to their respective assignments, Ninym was to investigate Levert while Raklum checked the surrounding area. However, Raklum shook his head with concern.

"Nothing worth reporting. General Levert appears to have a firm grip on the military. What about you?"

"Their defenses are tight, unfortunately, so it's been difficult. If only there was some sort of opportunity..."

It was at that moment that a carriage passed by the street in front of them. They watched as it stopped in front of Levert's mansion, where a certain figure got out—

"Holonyeh...?"

There was no mistaking him. It was Holonyeh, the vassal who had jumped ship from Marden to Cavarin and the one who Zeno despised for being a sellout.

"It's a good thing Lord Zeno isn't here. However... Hmm, two vassals of Cavarin, huh? It is not unusual to meet this way, but I do have my concerns."

"...Captain Raklum, please watch the perimeter. I'm not sure how far we'll be able to get, but let's give it a try."

Ninym took out a small telescope that she had on her. Tucking it into her breast pocket, she soundlessly scurried for a convenient location among a row of trees. The early spring leaves weren't exceptionally full, but the trees were decorated in celebration of the festival, giving her just enough concealment to hide.

"Well, then..." Ninym peeked through the telescope, directing the lens at Levert's mansion.

Before long, she spotted him through a window and confirmed the room he was in. As she continued to monitor him, Holonyeh appeared as if on cue. The two began to chat. She couldn't hear anything, but she could attempt to read their lips.

"As ordered... The building...blueprint...will be realized..."

The gears were turning in Ninym's head as she grasped bits and pieces of their conversation.

Holonyeh seemed to be conspiring to create some sort of plan. From the way they were acting, Levert was the one spearheading it.

"There is...your traitor...in the king's lineage..."

As Ninym continued to string their words together, Levert grew more heated, making his lips more difficult to read. But even picking up the smallest of hints left her completely floored.

"Without their prince...we can...take down Natra...?"

Ninym's heart constricted with an ominous premonition. The information exchanged in this conversation must intimately involve those close to her.

From here on out, she couldn't let a single word slip past her. However, just then a voice came from below.

"Lady Aide, people are coming; I'm afraid I must stop you short."

"Ngh…!"

When she looked around, a group of people were approaching from the other side of the street. It would quickly become a huge debacle if they were questioned. Not to mention that she was a Flahm—whether she was in disguise or not.

After not even a second's hesitation, she slid down the tree. They had to prioritize returning with the current information they had gathered over getting more. The two nodded to each other and quickly made their escape.

Gruyere Soljest. The king of the Soljest Kingdom and one of Levetia's Holy Elites.

Wein didn't have much intel on him. He hailed from a far-off nation, and Wein's Flahm information network couldn't fully operate there, since they were heavily oppressed in the West. But from the little information he had gleaned, Wein knew Gruyere was a brilliant strategist with an open-minded personality. There were always beautiful girls who waited on him, and more than anything—

He's über-fat, just like the rumors said.

Obese. Just really, really fat.

Wein had glanced at him briefly back at their first meeting, but the sheer magnitude of his weight was immense now that they were face-to-face.

He was tall, but his width was two or three people wide. He had the body of a small boulder. His clothing (which must have been custom-made) appeared to be of high-quality material, but they were stretched so far to their limits that there was the danger of a button popping off at just the slightest movement. Word had spread as far as Natra of the continent's biggest glutton—none other than Gruyere.

"I bet you thought I was fat just now, didn't you?"

"What? No, I would never." Wein panicked, wondering if Gruyere could read his micro-expressions, but the king gave a generous nod.

"Please, do not worry. All who meet me think the same thing." Gruyere guffawed before munching on the fruits that the ladies-in-waiting presented to him. The girls needed both hands to even hold the fruit, but for him, these fruits were bite-size.

"However, Crown Prince, I am not ashamed of this body in the least. Royalty and nobles need to be set apart from commoners. In other words, we can do what others cannot. I've assigned myself the role of enjoying this world's luxuries to the fullest."

"…I see. So that's why…"

It was no wonder he had a figure like that.

But Gruyere shook his head. "Oh, but do not misunderstand. For me, food is but a means to an end."

"What?"

"Yes… Crown Prince, when you think of luxury, what comes to mind?"

Wein thought for a few moments—not necessarily about the answer but if it was safe to answer honestly. In the end, he decided to go with the truth.

"Wearing fine clothes, eating good food, and sleeping with beautiful girls to my heart's content?"

Gruyere nodded. "I can sense a youthfulness in your answer. It warms my heart. Yes, I, too, used to spend all my time enjoying those pleasures. But one day, it hit me. If they had the money, even commoners could participate in these affairs."

Which goes the other way. If the royal family didn't have money, they couldn't do those things, either, Wein added internally.

"At the time, I had the opportunity to meet a renowned swordsman. His chiseled body was a marvel. Though impressed, I had another thought: that I should aim to be the exact opposite." Gruyere lifted a fat, swollen finger.

"I am fine with this pitiful body. I already cannot stand or use the facilities on my own. However, as a living creature, to destroy my body by my own will and inconvenience others as I maintain my existence... That is a luxury for which only I can aim."

"......"

Wein understood what Gruyere was trying to say, but he also had no idea what the hell he was going on about. Not that he would ever let it show on his face.

"Ah... The court doctor must be complaining his head off."

"Court doctor?!" Gruyere slapped his stomach as he laughed, which echoed with the tenor of a drum. "They fly into a panic and ask what's wrong if I neglect to finish my lunch. It's common knowledge that my body is too far gone. All I need are a persistent will, endless food, and my faith in god."

"Faith, huh? Pious, as expected of a Holy Elite... I would love to offer my prayers alongside you one day."

Wein got to the heart of the matter, and Gruyere's lips curled into a smile. It wasn't the same generous one as before but an expression of sharp intelligence and wit.

"Crown Prince, your body might be trim from a general lack of desire, but I can see you're keeping a beast within your stomach."

"What could that mean?"

"It's perfectly fine; I love greedy people. Throw in young talent, and that makes it all the more interesting. I love that you came to me first. I will endorse you as a Holy Elite."

"Oh... I'm most grateful."

There were currently seven Holy Elites. With Ordalasse's endorsement, this now made two votes. With just two more, Wein's name would be added to their ranks. However—

"There *is* one thing."

I knew it, Wein thought, steadying himself. Endorsing Wein didn't benefit Gruyere in any way. Therefore, he was obviously going to impose an extra condition.

But Wein would have never imagined what Gruyere would say next.

"How about ditching Ordalasse and teaming up with me?"

"…What?" Wein blinked a few times as Gruyere went on.

"I don't know what deal he's made with you, but that guy is on the decline. Targeting Marden's gold mine to win back his popularity and promising the Holy Elites a slice of the profits to avoid criticism is all fine and good. But the fact that he was unable to take the mine—because of *you*—and is already at a loss for how to handle Marden's leftovers means his end is not far off.

"…That is something," Wein added mildly, stowing away this new bit of information in the back of his mind. Gruyere had been the only one talking this entire time, but it was incredibly informative.

"When it comes to the trust the lords have in him as a Holy Elite, he's a sinking ship. You won't get anywhere with him. You'd be better off getting out while you still can."

"And I imagine that would not happen if I joined you, King Gruyere?"

"At the very least, it would sink slower."

"……"

Wein couldn't get a read on him. What was Gruyere thinking? It couldn't have been that he suddenly had taken a liking to Wein. Even if he had, there had to be something in it for the king.

Damn, things are crazy enough as it is…

It was the second day of the Festival of the Spirit. Not much time was left. On the other hand, it was too big of an opportunity to just ignore.

"I'm thankful for your proposal and consideration toward Natra. Be that as it may, it is a sudden matter that I cannot answer immediately. I ask for a bit more time to consider your offer."

"Watching young people fret gives me great pleasure. Take all the time you need—though you only have until tomorrow, when the Gathering of the Chosen takes place," Gruyere replied with a huge grin.

This bastard, Wein thought as he internally clicked his tongue.

"Well then, we've talked at length. I'll be retiring now. I assume you have other places to be."

"Yes, I'll be meeting with Duke Lozzo and Director Caldmellia of the Gospel Bureau."

"The Artist Duke and God's Mistress, huh?" Gruyere gave a wry smile. "Well, if we're talking about eccentric types—reckless enough to actually try to set up a meeting with you—I guess they're the only ones, other than me... Don't drop your guard for even a second. One of them is sane, but the other is a broken soul."

"I will keep that in mind."

Gruyere nodded, and he turned toward the food the servants offered him. He was making it clear the conversation was over, but Wein pushed on.

"Might I ask one more question, King Gruyere?"

"Yeah? What?"

"What do you think of Marden, the nation destroyed by Cavarin?"

At this question, Zeno's shoulders twitched as she stood behind Wein as an attendant.

Gruyere must have been surprised at this question because he stared at Wein, searching for a motive. Finally, he shrugged—though he couldn't do it very well with all the abundant fat layered around his neck.

"In a nutshell, I have no interest in it. It was a country that was headed for destruction all along. Now that they lost the gold mine to Natra, they're a worthless wreck."

"...But Marden's Liberation Front is active there."

"That's just a troop of fools who put off fixing their country until it was destroyed—even though they had the time and opportunity to change their ways before all this. They'll disappear in time."

"……"

Gruyere gave his scathing evaluation with nonchalance. With no emotional ties to the matter, it was clearly as objective as an opinion could be.

"I don't know what you're hung up on, but I'm sure you have more important things to think about. Look at what's in front of you."

"…You're right. Thank you very much, King Gruyere."

Wein bowed deeply and excused himself from Gruyere's mansion.

"Um… Zeno?"

As they boarded the carriage waiting for them outside the mansion and headed toward the next Holy Elite, Wein called out to the girl who mournfully hung her head.

"I won't say you shouldn't worry about it… But you have to remember that's just what King Gruyere thinks. It's not like all the Holy Elites will feel the same way."

"Yes…" Zeno just barely responded, and there was no strength in it.

"Opportunity… Time… Yes, I had those things. Or I should have, and yet…" Zeno whimpered, quietly condemning herself.

Wein looked at Zeno and gave up on trying to intervene. He had a mountain of other matters to think about.

The least he could do was pray that the next Holy Elite would have some good news for her.

Steel Lozzo. The duke of one of the West's larger nations, the Kingdom of Vanhelio.

He had to be somewhere in his mid-twenties, which meant he was fairly young, and his clean-cut looks charmed all the ladies. He was skilled in politics—and excelled with a pen and the sword.

He was most famous for being a supporter of the arts, and it was said that aspiring artists from across the continent gathered in his domain. He seemed to be everything anyone could possibly expect of a young nobleman—but within that shining profile were inappropriate rumors that dogged him.

"—It is an honor to meet you, Prince Wein. I understand that we met the other day, but this is the first time that we've been formally introduced."

Steel greeted his guest with a warm smile and a handshake.

"The pleasure is all mine, Duke Lozzo. Rumors of the renowned Artist Duke have spread to the far corners of Natra."

"Ha-ha-ha. Then I would be remiss to not mention that my own nation has heard of your bravery. Many of the artists I support are inspired by anecdotes of your deeds of driving off Marden with a small force. They are currently in the midst of painting these scenes. As soon as they are finished, I shall send you a few of their works."

"Well... That is kind of you to offer, though slightly embarrassing."

"Ha-ha... It is the fate of heroes to be beloved by the masses in all their various forms."

Their conversation sparked, as though they were old friends having a familiar chat. It must have been because they were relatively close in age. The start to the meeting could not have gone any smoother.

"Duke Lozzo, I had been hoping to ask you if we ever had the chance to meet, but for what reason do you support the arts?"

In this era, artists were joined at the hip with those of influence. Across the continent, it wasn't uncommon for people to starve to death. How could artists avoid this fate when they weren't contributing to manufacturing or producing a product? The answer was to receive a salary under a wealthy benefactor. As for the people in power, they always hungered for more amusement. These pieces of art were largely to relieve their boredom. For this reason, it wasn't odd at all for the rich to support the livelihood and work of their favorite artists. However, Steel was on a whole different level. With an entire city under his domain, a majority of the people there were involved in some form of artistic creation.

"The reason, huh…? If I must give one, I would say it is because I am searching."

"Searching for what?"

"The inspiration that will make me an artist."

The heck? Wein couldn't quite catch his meaning, and Steel went on theatrically.

"When we encounter something that moves us, we gravitate toward it: a stage for a dancer, a pen for a writer, an instrument for a musician, a paintbrush for an artist. Inspiration is the source of the arts—"

"Those are the words of Rahel, the artist who took the world by storm two hundred years ago."

"So you know him. You're absolutely right," Steel replied happily. "This quote by Rahel waxes poetic about artistic roots, but it is here I discovered a new truth."

"And what's that?"

"An artist can be created."

Wein thought about that for a second before understanding. If inspiration made an artist, what was preventing a man-made source of inspiration from making them, too?

"When I realized this, I delved deeper into the meaning of inspiration. I came to the conclusion that inspiration is composed of two elements."

"Which are?"

"The first is accomplishment. I issued an assignment to many of my subjects. Once they completed it, they had a sense of achievement that they used to create songs, paintings, and pottery. I then observed the quality of the finished work—by gauging how much it touched me."

Steel looked almost intoxicated as he recalled those pieces.

"I gave them all the reward they could ever wish for: golden cups; remote locations untouched by human eyes; kind, beautiful wives… Those rewards became the impetus for the next trial, and then I had them strive for even greater achievements…!"

"Ah… I see. But what is the other factor?"

Detecting his wild fervor, Wein forcefully tried to get the conversation back on track.

A moment later, Wein regretted his decision.

"Loss." Steel's eyes shifted ominously. His cheery nature turned to its polar opposite, and the light disappeared from his eyes.

"Gain and loss. Those are what truly changes the human heart."

A decidedly terrible question came to Wein's mind.

"…Duke Lozzo, have you *tested that out, too?*"

"*Why wouldn't I?*" Steel said easily. "I've trampled heirlooms more precious than life itself underfoot, burned the nostalgic scenery of one's birthplace to ashes, killed wives and children waiting for their husbands and fathers to return right before the artists' eyes."

"……"

"You know, those artists with murdered families created the best work. What do you think happened when I gave a paintbrush and canvas to those who cursed me, raged at their own powerlessness, and suffered from self-loathing? After they ripped off their own scalp and painted the canvas with their flesh and blood, they ended up stabbing their own throats with the brush. It was… Ah, truly inspirational work."

Steel Lozzo was massacring innocent people for his amusement.

Wein had heard the rumors that Steel reeked of blood—and he saw now they were not entirely unfounded.

Steel continued. "I have always wanted to be an artist, but nothing in the natural world ever inspired me. I only found satisfaction in admiring man-made products—buildings and paintings."

"…And that's why you've gathered the artists."

"Yes. By making them compete and giving them inspiration, I want them to give birth to work that would unconsciously give me the desire to create… That is my goal. What do you think? A very small thing to ask, isn't it?"

"I am unable to comment on whether it is 'small'…but it is unique."

Wein chose his words carefully, and Steel smiled as he took his hand.

"How wonderful… When I talk about this to others, most reject me, but you're different, Prince. I knew you would be. You have the makings of a true artist."

Wein almost asked if that was a compliment, but he held himself back.

"I will help you become a Holy Elite. The current members hardly understood the arts, but we can change that. Why, I say we should imbue the entire Western world with culture!" yelled Steel.

With a loud gasp, he suddenly came back to himself.

"Pardon me, I have not met anyone who has understood me in so long that I seem to have gotten a bit excited."

"…Please, do not mind me. Your recommendation means everything."

Steel nodded in affirmation. "I'm certain you have other matters to attend to, Prince Wein. I'm reluctant, but let us end here for today. Please come visit me anytime."

"I'm grateful for your kindness, Duke Lozzo. Thank you very much for today."

Wein and Steel both exchanged a firm handshake.

—DUDE. He is out of his mind.

Back in the carriage, Wein let out a huge sigh of relief that he'd been able to leave Steel's mansion in one piece.

I have to team up with that guy? Seriously? What kind of punishment is this...?

Wein looked over at Zeno, whose face was pale again—though, this time it was for a different reason altogether: Steel's terrible eccentricity.

"Sorry, Zeno, I couldn't find the right timing to bring up the Liberation Front."

"...Please do not worry over it... I'm willing to bet... I mean, I'm absolutely certain he has not been paying attention to us at all."

Wein didn't say anything but agreed. As long as the Remnant Army wasn't a group of pioneering artists, it seemed like Steel couldn't care less. Even if by some chance they were the best artists in the world, Marden would likely try to help those artists escape with them back to their own territory.

Even then, this was a painful position for Zeno to be in. For her, it was the same as cutting off lifelines one by one.

If the last person was what they'd been told, she would be just as much trouble as the last two.

I hope she proves the rumors wrong.

Wein held on to this small hope, even though he knew it would never come to life. Wein's rumbling carriage continued on.

"...I see... You've been outcast at school... I imagine you suffered a great deal."

At the center of the room were a fine woman and a young girl.

The young girl hung her head, eyes brimming with tears, and the woman stroked her hair affectionately.

"Miss Caldmellia… What should I do…?" asked the young girl, seeking guidance from the older woman.

"Do you understand why they are ostracizing you?"

"It must be… It must be because I'm a bad person…"

"No, you have done nothing wrong," Caldmellia consoled softly. "I imagine they see you only as a shadow in their hearts."

"A…shadow?" repeated the girl, teary-eyed in confusion.

"Yes, you are not a person but a shadow. That is why no one comes to save you—even as you cry and scream and call out for help… After all, people do not experience heartache from hurting shadows."

"So how do I stop being one? How can I get them to see me as human?" she screeched, heartbroken.

Caldmellia gave a smile like the Holy Mother.

"—Create a vortex of despair," she explained, as if it were the only way in the world. "Drag the ringleaders, their followers, and everyone who saw and turned the other way into a miserable vortex of your own imagining. Afterward, throw yourself in as well."

Caldmellia gently touched the girl's cheek. "By overcoming that despair alongside them, your existence will pierce through their hearts, tinged with the physicality of flesh and blood. Once that comes to pass, no one will tyrannize you."

"B-but… Will I be forgiven for my deeds?"

"Yes." Caldmellia's voice was like a mother singing a lullaby to her child.

"Because you will be the one doing the forgiving. Isn't that right? You will forgive those who oppressed you and transcend despair together. Then the other party may forgive you, too."

"But…if by some chance…I'm not forgiven…"

"Then," Caldmellia said, peering straight into the eyes of the girl, who was unable to look away. "They are animals, not people.

Animals who do wrong by man must not live. It is fine to nip their lives short."

"……"

"It is all right. There is no need to fear. I will be with you. Be courageous, take your despair, and—"

"—*Koff!*" echoed a very fake cough, which had to be deliberate, from behind them.

In her surprise, the girl stepped away from Caldmellia. As she turned around, she saw Wein and the others in the entrance.

"Ah… Um, thank you very much for your time! Please excuse me, Lady Caldmellia…!" blubbered the girl, slipping past Wein to flee the room.

Wein watched her run off, then turned to Caldmellia.

"It appears I have caught you in the middle of something. Forgive my ill manners, Lady Caldmellia."

"Hee-hee, please think nothing of it. Thank you for coming, Crown Prince."

Prompted by Caldmellia, Wein took a seat, keeping alert while staring fixedly at the woman across from him.

This is the rumored Caldmellia, huh…?

She was the director of Levetia's Gospel Bureau. Her position, plain and simple, made her the aide to Levetia's leader, the Holy King. The role was originally supposed to be held by a Holy Elite, but most held an earthly position—kings and nobles—making it difficult to stay by the Holy King's side permanently. That was why the Gospel Bureau was formed. They had a long history: They occasionally acted publicly on behalf of the Holy King, and these days they had an authority rivaling that of the Holy Elites. The one to attend on behalf of the Holy King at this last Gathering of the Chosen had been the director of the Gospel Bureau, Caldmellia.

The West is already misogynistic. An interpretation of Levetia's sacred book means women aren't often accepted in high positions. And yet…

Caldmellia had risen up to director of the Gospel Bureau, the highest position in Levetia that one can achieve without relation to the founder, Levetia, or the lead disciples.

She'd been called a political monster by some. Wein found none more suited for this nickname.

"…Was that young girl from the nobility?"

Wein's way of life was steering clear of troublemakers, but now that he was already involved, there wasn't much else to be done. He steeled himself.

"No, she's a commoner."

"Oh, I see… Then do you normally preach to them?"

"My role is to save the troubled and guide them to Levetia. As a believer, it is only natural that I hold my hand out to my fellow brethren."

"How inspiring, Lady Caldmellia. If the founder could see you, I'm certain Levetia would be pleased." Wein doled out praise, exchanging meaningless pleasantries as he tried to find a lead for his next move.

As if to say she had no interest in this exchange, Caldmellia cut straight to the point.

"By the way, Crown Prince, you've come here today because you wish for me to support your candidacy to become a Holy Elite, right?"

"…Yes, though I am aware it is an imprudent request. But it is a necessary one."

He had planned to go about this with more caution, but Wein changed course immediately. His opponent was strong-willed, so he decided to try pressuring her.

"As you know, our country receives refugees from both the East and the West. Many are in search of salvation, but at the same time, they still believe in barbaric false idols."

"Do you mean to say the people of Natra are heathens?"

"No, it is simply all they've ever known. In this land, Levetia is the one true religion. Be that as it may, the teachings themselves don't hold any value unless they touch people's hearts. The one sin in this entire situation lies squarely on our shoulders—for not fully spreading the true word across the land before they were born."

Caldmellia thought for just a moment.

"Well then, are you saying you will change their hearts as a Holy Elite?"

"Precisely. The confusion that troubles the people of Natra is a failure of my own doing. Thus, I wish for the chance to atone as a Holy Elite. Under the banner of Levetia, I'm sure the people of Natra will immediately reconsider their beliefs and be reborn as followers."

"But their hearts have already been captured by evil. Can you really purify them?"

"Discovered by angels, Saint Loran said, 'Believing all people have the right to be saved is the first step to salvation.' I believe in the people of Natra. Won't you believe in them as well, Lady Caldmellia...?!"

He internally patted his own back for his silver tongue as he awaited her reply.

"...I understand your heart well, Crown Prince," Caldmellia said with a gentle smile. "Please forgive me for my incendiary questions. To be a Holy Elite is to enter a sacred position. It comes with great influence and power. Those who are thoughtless and cruel could cause chaos if appointed. However, it appears my worries have been unfounded."

"In that case..."

"Yes, as one with the full authority to act on behalf of His Holiness, I accept you as worthy of becoming a Holy Elite... But I do have one condition."

"Your wish is my command." Wein did not falter. He had

assumed this might happen. In fact, her manner signified she was leaning toward compliance.

"It is regarding King Ordalasse. This last war between Natra and Marden was in order to save Marden from tyrannical rule, right? They say it is a feat worthy of becoming a Holy Elite."

That wasn't true at all, of course. It was just a justification added after the fact. Both Wein and the Holy Elites were aware of this. Why was Caldmellia bringing this up now? The gears in Wein's head started to turn.

She's trying to confirm it was a holy war… In other words, she wants to know if it was a conflict over ideology…and not one that was for worldly gain… If she's attacking me from that standpoint, then… It must be about the mine!

It was entirely plausible that she would demand the gold mine as contribution to Levetia in return for helping him become a Holy Elite. Wein began to quickly consider the pros and cons of this situation, but he couldn't have guessed her next comment.

"—In that case, you must *completely* save them, or I cannot offer my support."

"What…?" Wein spoke, hurriedly swallowing his involuntary rush of confusion. "'Save them' all…? Natra fought alongside Cavarin to take the royal capital of Marden, and—"

"But they're still alive—the *Remnants*."

Wein felt a chill run down his spine.

"The Remnants of Marden… I hear those who oppress the followers of Levetia want to continue resisting us. I imagine the pious experience sleepless nights, fearing when the devil's hand will shoot out to oppress them again. To return peace to our believers, we must destroy them completely, put their bodies on display, and toss them into a raging fire… Don't you agree?"

Caldmellia did have a point. However, that was all she had—a point to prove but no marked benefit.

Nothing more. Crushing the remaining forces of Marden was already an established policy—even without Caldmellia's prompting. To exchange that for his candidacy as a Holy Elite didn't make any sense.

I can think of two things: One, Caldmellia somehow benefits from Natra going to war and suppressing Marden's rebels, and I simply don't know why yet. Two—

"Hmm… Is something the matter?" Caldmellia suddenly called out to someone behind Wein.

Standing there was Zeno, who looked on the verge of collapse, judging by her complexion.

"If you are feeling unwell, feel free to sit in this chair."

Upon witnessing her seemingly innocent behavior, Wein was convinced.

Caldmellia knew. She knew members of Marden's Remnant Army were in his delegation. She had figured out their goal was to help liberate Marden—and that there was a high probability a member of the Remnant Army would be present at this visit.

That had to be why she had come up with an idea: *I think I'll toy with them a little.*

I seeeeeeee. A game, huh?

There was something Wein had thought when he'd heard her preaching to the girl. But this was enough to convince him.

There were people in the world who would steer events into devastation and chaos for no other reason than personal amusement. They had no fear of destruction or desire for profit.

And this woman Caldmellia was one of them. For her, the position of Holy Elite was nothing more than a tool to make things more interesting for her.

"P-please do not worry yourself over me… It is nothing of concern…"

"There is no need to put on a brave face. I am sure you're in pain just thinking about the persecution of the devout followers in your former Marden?"

"N-no, I…"

Caldmellia reached out to Zeno. "It is all right; you have nothing to fear. After all, the crown prince will save them—"

"Pardon me, Lady Caldmellia."

Before the hand could reach her, Wein had embraced Zeno.

"You are right. Returning the former Marden to stability should be our first priority. However, this is a joint effort with the Kingdom of Cavarin. I cannot answer at my own discretion. I ask that I might be able to converse with King Ordalasse and give my answer at a later point in time."

"Goodness…" Caldmellia's brows knit together in disappointment, but she soon switched to a fleeting smile.

"If that is to be the case, let us wait until the meeting tomorrow."

"I appreciate it. I apologize, but as I must prepare to meet with King Ordalasse, I'm afraid we must end here for today."

"I would have enjoyed speaking with you more, Crown Prince, but alas… Your companion may visit anytime for respite."

"I appreciate your concern. Well then, by your leave."

Forcibly ending the conversation, Wein left the room with Zeno.

"Hee-hee. Oh, how flustered he became."

Watching from the window as Wein's carriage drove off with his entourage, Caldmellia giggled and turned around. A man was standing there.

"Will this serve as revenge for your lost arm, Owl?"

If Wein had still been in the room, he would have been surprised indeed. After all, this one-armed man named Owl had crossed swords with Wein in an Eastern city due to a certain incident.

"You enjoy yourself too much, Lady Caldmellia. I was concerned whether that one believer might grow violent."

"That would have been interesting."

Owl closed his eyes at her attitude that spoke of little danger. He was well aware of her disposition but found it frustrating regardless. Not to mention there was still another matter at hand.

"…Will you actually support adding the crown prince to the ranks of the Holy Elites?"

"Yes, and gladly, if he properly kills Marden's leftovers," Caldmellia asserted with a nod.

Owl went on. "With all due respect, that prince is dangerous. If he gains a position of power in the West, he will most certainly do you wrong, Lady Caldmellia."

"And that is a good thing, right?" she said, as if it were only obvious. "I was worried about our new plan, now that our old scheme to incite disturbances in the East and spread chaos here has been foiled. But now the West will be ravaged by fire, too."

Caldmellia smiled—even now, her expression could be called nothing less than the face of a Holy Mother, which was why it reeked of a peculiar sense of artifice.

Owl no longer had any grounds for complaint.

"And how is Ibis?" she asked.

"Operating as planned. She says the battle formation will be complete before the end of the festival."

"I am glad to hear it. It is our highly anticipated festival. We must make it as exciting as possible. If there is anything you require, please send word."

"Understood…"

Owl exited noiselessly. Caldmellia again looked outside the window. Thinking of the departed carriage, she almost sang to herself.

"Hee-hee… May you not make it in time."

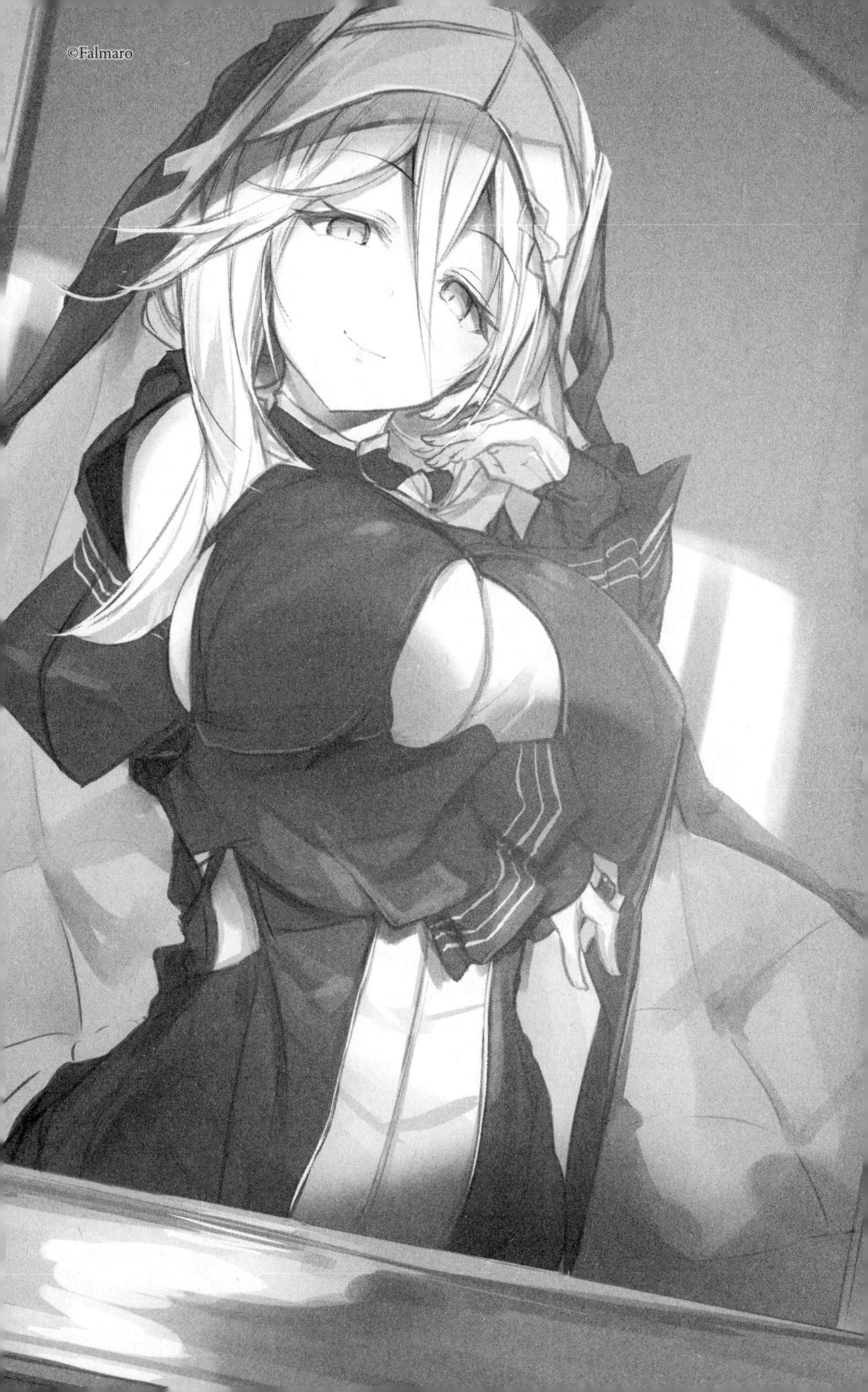
©Falmaro

The mood was subdued in the carriage. Zeno hung her head word-lessly, and even Wein couldn't find the right thing to say.

As they were, Zeno only had one choice: kill Wein and call off the ties between Natra and Cavarin. That would buy her enough time to work through a contingency plan. Now that Wein and Zeno were in this private space together, one could say it was her greatest chance.

But Zeno didn't intend to go through with it. She was in despair. This was one of those rare situations where a single word perfectly described her emotional state.

"...I can see it was a half-hearted dream." Zeno spoke in frag-ments. "I thought if we showed signs of distress and called for aid, we would receive help from somewhere in the world...but I was naive..."

"...Well, that's true."

Things would have panned out differently if the Remnant Army had strengthened relations with foreign nations earlier. The world might have responded if they'd been able to take back the capital from Cavarin. If only they had done this... If only they had the foresight to plan that—

There were infinite other ways they could have handled that situ-ation. But there was no changing it now.

"I was surprised myself. To think the Holy Elites would be a bunch of shams."

"Yes... I was shocked."

"Especially Caldmellia. Did you know? According to records, she is a woman in her sixties."

Zeno widened her blank eyes. "...I thought she was in her thirties."

"Me too… Either the name has been inherited for generations or she's just as good at disguise as the Flahm. I wonder which one it is."

"…Either way, she's a monster… My father was completely…"

As Wein listened to Zeno talk partly to herself, someone suddenly called out. "—Your Highness, over there."

"Hmm? …Stop the carriage."

It creaked to a halt. When Wein looked outside the window, he saw Raklum standing there.

"Your Highness, I am glad to see you are safe."

"You too. Just on your way back?"

"Yes. I have returned to compile the information obtained by me and the Lady Aide."

"Great. Hop in."

"Understood. Please excuse me."

Raklum climbed in, and they soon set off once again.

"Anything of note?"

"I did not get much intel, but the Lady Aide uncovered vital information."

"I see… Good work. Let's talk about it more once we get back."

Raklum nodded obediently before glancing at Zeno next to him. From that mournful face, he was able to guess how the meetings had gone.

"By the way, Raklum… Is that a book you have there?" Wein pointed at the book poking out of his leather bag.

"Yes, I found it at a bookbinding shop on the road. To study Levetia's sacred texts as you suggested."

"That's the right attitude… Do I see another one?"

"Yes, I was introduced to a book that has been recently growing in popularity in the West with everyone from nobles to merchants. It intrigued me, and I bought it on a whim. The title is *The Dignity of Imperial Court*, and—"

"You can just toss that one."

"Underst... What?" Raklum stopped himself from giving his reflexive reply when he processed Wein's words. He blinked a few times. "I will do as you say, Your Highness, but..."

Raklum was absolutely loyal to Wein, meaning he had no choice but to follow his orders. However, he also knew that Wein was not the type of person to treat a book with disdain for no reason.

"Do you mind if I ask why?"

"Because I'm the one who wrote it."

Raklum was left dumbfounded.

"To be precise, I drafted it and asked a skilled Flahm author to write it. We circulated the final book throughout the West. As for when it was published... I guess that was before my exchange period in the Empire."

"I see... But as your vassal, shouldn't I read—?"

"No need." Wein abruptly cut him off. "I'll give you a summary: The nobles are required to be loyal, uphold chivalry, serve their monarch with heart and soul. They are to appreciate song and dance, be prolific in poetry and love, and spend extravagantly. Frugality and honorable poverty are not meant for those of true noble birth." Wein sneered.

"What do you think about this aristocratic ideal?"

"Ah yes... I might say it seems the noblest of noble."

"You got that right." Wein's lips curled. "The book affirms the nobles—encouraging them to be stagnant and expressing that they're already wonderful. Of course, it's been warmly received by them. It praises them for doing nothing. But there's one trap in there. About money."

"Money?"

"To cast aside frugality. To frame honorable poverty as sin. It essentially tells nobles to not keep track of their spending habits. It scorns budgeting, financing their money. As the reader, you start to align yourself with these values."

"But wouldn't that be too impractical in reality?"

"Not really. Humans tend to be all or nothing when it comes to a belief. It's not easy to believe in one part of the book and not the other."

Ninety percent of the book affirmed their lifestyle. Denying the section about their finances would feel the same as rejecting the rest of the book. That's why avid readers were almost always unable to disagree with the lessons on money.

"To begin with, bookkeeping is a plain and boring task. By claiming that they are somehow exempt from it—that it is, in fact, *bad* to do it—they start to believe it. The water seeks its own level."

Raklum gave a grunt of consideration. He wasn't completely convinced, but Wein did have a point. However, he had a more basic question at hand.

"I understand what you are saying, Your Highness. But why did you circulate such a book in the West?"

"Isn't it obvious?" Wein's smile was both gentle and cruel. "To totally mess up the West."

"……" Raklum involuntarily caught his breath. That was a quiet viciousness exuding from the normally kind prince.

"There are three requirements for smooth operations: reward proportionate to the work, reputation, and punishment." Wein raised three fingers on his hand. "Especially when it comes to bookkeeping, it's easy to be dishonest. The responsible party needs perseverance and professional ethics. But in this book, I mocked this activity. If the value of a position goes down, the reputation and reward will decrease as well. What do you think happens then?"

"…Nobody will want to do it."

"Exactly. By nature, managing their finances is essential for nobles. In fact, they have to be the ones *taking* the initiative. But the book condemns it. Which means they'll foist this task on someone else. The only people who would take up a thankless and unrewarding job are those without status or ambition."

"……!" Raklum understood what Wein was getting at. Wein nodded and continued.

"But it's not like you can expect them to have patience or decent morals. Dishonest deeds come as second nature to them. There will be frequent miscalculations, and the nobles start to show contempt for accountants, increasing punishment more and more, which will further exacerbate a shortage of capable personnel."

This would ultimately cause the affected nobility to be clueless about what was in their own coffers. If that happened, it wouldn't be long before they collapsed. As a cruel trick, desperate nobles would impose heavier taxes, which would drive away merchants, and starving citizens would disrupt the public order, leading to ruin. Who and where would they scrape money away from to keep the soldiers in check? There was no guaranteed future for such a fiefdom.

"—I don't really know how well it actually worked," Wein admitted without care.

"Is—is that so…?"

"It's only one book, after all. It seems to have picked up some underground influence, but it could very well not stick and become forgotten in the public consciousness. We'll cross that bridge when we come to it, I guess."

"Is it okay to handle it in this way?"

"Yes. This plan is working out the best for now, but I've got little traps set up elsewhere. If this one doesn't work out, we'll just redirect our energy somewhere else." Wein laughed easily.

He had written it before studying in the Empire. In other words, a boy who was hardly a teenager had devised and carried out this plan. Raklum couldn't help but shiver in fear.

"Anyway, now you know why you don't need to read it, right?"

"Yes… But I cannot toss aside a book written by Your Highness. While I vow not to read through it, please forgive me for keeping it on my person."

Hmm, Wein thought for a moment. In this era, books were considered precious items. It would be harsh to tell him to chuck it.

"Very well. Do as you like. You can read it if you want. But don't take it to heart."

"Yes, thank you very much." Raklum bowed deeply.

Raklum suddenly took notice of Zeno's behavior. She was staring at Wein with fearful eyes.

He had no way of knowing this was the same look she had given the Holy Elites.

When Wein got back, Ninym was waiting for him as usual.

Zeno said she wished to be left with her thoughts for a while, leaving Wein, who listened to Ninym's and Raklum's reports, in his room.

"Hmm... A secret meeting between Levert and Holonyeh, huh?"

"Yes. We cannot come to any conclusions, as I was unable to grasp the entire conversation that passed between them, but their aim is..."

"Attacking us here. And taking my life," Wein finished for her.

"Yes..."

Levert had always advocated for bold attacks against Natra. If they assassinated Wein before an alliance between Natra and Cavarin could be formed, war would be unavoidable.

"...And our accommodations were too small to fit all the guards."

Raklum nodded. "Yes. In addition, Holonyeh was the one to guide us here. There is also a possibility he was the one who made the arrangements."

Their aim was obviously to disperse Wein's forces and make it easier to attack. Thinking back, they had argued about the number of attendants before they'd even left Natra. If the attack on their journey here had been under Levert's orders, there was a good chance it was meant to put an easy end to Wein.

"Holonyeh's goal must be to get Levert to owe him a favor—instead of focusing on King Ordalasse, who is slipping from power as we speak. I imagine he's aiming to be placed in charge of the mine when they steal it back."

Ninym agreed with Wein's prediction. "Holonyeh must have been the one managing the mine, back when it was Marden territory. With his know-how, this proposal would be in the bag. I can almost guarantee it."

Wein sighed. "I have to admit it's pretty clever. I'd hire him if he ever floated over to Natra."

"Really?"

"It's more realistic to manage someone who is skilled and immoral than pray to the heavens for someone who is skilled *and* moral."

Ninym and Raklum gave each other a look.

"In any case, I get where Levert's coming from now. Next, Ordalasse. I think I already have him figured out, too." Wein went on. "Ordalasse has tried to cling to his position using his bloodline, but he's starting to hit the limits of that method. He's losing the hearts of the people. He must have seen the gold mine as the edge he needed to reclaim some stability. To prevent criticism, he promised to loan the Holy Elites some money and laid the groundwork, timing his invasion while Natra and Marden were busy fighting. When Marden fell, he would profit while others did the fighting for him."

"However," he continued. "This plan fell through. Marden was defeated, and Natra took the mine."

Ninym folded her arms. "From the start, Marden was just as poor as Natra. It didn't have anything of value outside the mine, so this change in course must have caused King Ordalasse a great deal of trouble."

"That said, if he threw away this new territory, he would lose even more momentum," Raklum observed with a grunt.

Wein nodded. "Then, add in the resistance of the Remnant

Army. Cavarin's casualties and expenses kept blowing up—without ever seeing any increased profit. To make matters worse for him, his position as a Holy Elite deteriorated because he was unable to pay them as promised. That was when…"

Wein pointed at himself. "…Ordalasse zeroed in on me. By dangling the recommendation for the Holy Elite in front of me, he wanted to make me owe him a debt of gratitude while also strengthening his faction."

After this upcoming meeting, Ordalasse would probably ask to buy off gold from the mine for cheap. That was how he would ultimately improve his own standing.

That's about all the information we have so far. I've got a couple of options.

He could continue working with King Ordalasse and aim to be a Holy Elite. Or he could keep pretending to be on King Ordalasse's side while secretly teaming up with Gruyere. Or he could give up on becoming a Holy Elite now and just go home.

The issue was deciding the option that would offer him the greatest advantage. As Wein sunk deeper in thought, a knock came at the door.

"Pardon me."

Zeno appeared. Everyone in the room was a little surprised to see her.

She'd been in a trance, a stupor, when they first got back, but now her eyes burned with purpose. She kneeled before Wein.

"If I may, I have a favor to ask of you."

"And what's that?"

"Please allow me to accompany you to your audience with King Ordalasse."

Wein wasn't surprised. He'd been thinking there was a good chance she would make this request.

"Do you understand the situation you're in right now?"

"…I do. I can no longer hope for the aid of the Holy Elites, and an alliance between Natra and Cavarin is close at hand. The lives of those in the Liberation Front are in a precarious state."

"Then you must know why I can't bring you along… I can't let you assassinate King Ordalasse."

Taking advantage of the chaos in the wake of Ordalasse's death and launching a counterattack was the only choice the Remnant Army had left.

"No, you are *mistaken*," Zeno said, as if cutting off his thoughts. "I have no intention of trying to assassinate him."

"Oh…? Then why do you want to come with me?"

"So that the Liberation Front may form an alliance with Natra."

Everyone's eyes widened except for Zeno's.

"And why should Natra join the Liberation Front?"

"I do not know!" Zeno shouted.

Wein was confused by this unexpected take, but Zeno spoke without hesitation.

"But we may be able to find out! There is still time before the Gathering of the Chosen tomorrow! Until then, I will search for the reason with all my strength!"

It was a will of fire. While it was no more than an ardent—and reckless—proposal, most wouldn't have been able to help nodding in agreement when faced with such passion.

"No can do."

But Wein was not one to bend to words with no substance.

"I commend your spirit. But that doesn't obligate me to bring you along, and I don't see the value in it. To get straight to the point, I don't trust you."

It was a merciless rejection, but Zeno's heart would not be broken.

"Are you saying you do not trust me?"

"That's right. Is there some reason why I should?"

"No, I do not have anything so convenient. However…" Zeno took a breath. "…You previously said, Your Highness, that trust only has value because there's the potential of betrayal. And I'd like you to take a chance on me." She balled up both fists, looking forward courageously.

"……" Wein remained silent for a moment as he looked at Zeno, then suddenly flashed her a small smile.

"You can promise not to kill him, right? Taking out a sword in the middle of a meeting is only acceptable for an uncultured barbarian."

"I promise."

"…All right. I'll bring you along."

Zeno's face lit up as she beamed. "Th-thank you very much!"

"It's still too early for that. You still have to show me the new path you're proposing for the future." Wein had a somewhat amused look. "Raklum, it's a bit early, but prepare to head to the castle. Ninym, reorganize the defenses according to the likelihood of Levert's attacks and confirm the readiness of our escape route."

""Understood!"" The two loyal retainers set off with purpose.

Not long after, Wein, Raklum, and Zeno headed to their audience with King Ordalasse.

…I wonder what will actually happen.

Left behind in the mansion, Ninym called out orders to strengthen the defenses as she recalled Zeno's fiery words. The fact that she had said them at all made it clear the Remnant Army was in a dire situation. For Natra to reject a potential alliance with Cavarin and align with them instead, there would have to be a significant reason. Ninym doubted Zeno could actually deliver on that promise.

Personally, she absolutely hoped Zeno would propose something that Wein could accept. Both as a person and as a Flahm, she had her own opinions on Wein becoming a Holy Elite of Levetia, a religion that discriminated against her people.

It'd be nice if there was some sudden change, but…

She let herself sink into thought, allowing her mind to run wild, but she found no epiphany waiting for her.

And aside from being unable to think of an alternate plan, she had no right to defy her master's decision.

I guess I have no choice but to accept the results of the meeting—whatever they might be.

Ninym awaited Wein and the others' return.

"Hey, Prince Wein. Right on time."

Upon entering the castle, Wein was shown into not the audience hall but one of several parlors.

"With the topic being what it is, I thought we'd talk in here where there won't be any prying ears."

"I have no objections. However…" Wein trailed off, sitting down on the sofa and looking straight ahead, behind Ordalasse—at Holonyeh, who was standing there.

"Why is Lord Holonyeh here?"

"Ah, he's a newcomer, but he's got a real knack for it. He's been assisting me in various matters lately."

"I see," Wein responded in the socially acceptable way while moaning internally.

Cavarin had a long history—even though it had nothing on Natra. Of course, this meant many of the vassals had inherited their positions. Which meant there was something off about the king keeping a newcomer like Holonyeh by his side.

When Holonyeh had visited Natra, Wein had been impressed that he had managed to butter up the king enough to become an envoy. In truth, his cunning couldn't be denied. But even Wein had not imagined that the someone with almost nothing in the way of blood relations had managed to get this close to the seat of power.

This was the "sinking ship" Gruyere was talking about…

Wein's impression of Ordalasse tanked. He glanced behind the king. Zeno was standing in the back. He had heard from Ninym that Zeno hated Holonyeh. There was some concern she might run wild—but surprisingly, she was acting very calm, looking down, her breath steady, holding herself together.

We should be fine.

There were only four people in the room. Led by Raklum, the guards were waiting outside. If there were signs of any trouble, he had planned to force Zeno out of the room, but from the look of things, he could probably keep her close by.

"Well then, Prince Wein. Let's start things off. How did the meetings with the other Holy Elites go?"

"I was given a number of conditions, but overall, the responses were favorable. With yourself included, I will have the majority vote."

"Wonderful." Ordalasse gave a look of admiration. "To think befriending those wretches would give us these results. I can see you carry the blood of Caleus."

"Levetia's top disciple, known for being taciturn? I have heard I carry that blood, but that era is distant enough to feel somewhat unreal to me."

"Why, it is the reason you've gotten this far. There is no doubt you carry on an outstanding lineage, Prince. Ah, it's actually too bad. If I had a daughter your age, I'd marry her off to you."

While Wein was not in the least disappointed over Ordalasse's statement, he did have a question.

"If memory serves, isn't there a queen of Cavarin…?"

He couldn't be sure of the accuracy of this information, seeing that there wasn't much record of her entering the realm of politics, but Ordalasse should have had a few sons and daughters around Wein's own age.

Just as he was thinking maybe they had fallen victim to some disease, Ordalasse shook his head.

"Ah, those aren't my children."

"…Not your children?"

"In spite of the excellent teachers I hired, none of them produced any results. There was no way they could be mine…" Ordalasse got that far, then stopped.

"Oh, it seems I've gone off track." He sounded troubled. "My unfaithful ex-wife was executed, so you won't have to suffer the presence of such a vile being, Prince. Please do not worry."

"…Did you have definite proof?"

"Proof?" Ordalasse's lips turned into an odd frown. "What a thing to say. They did not produce results worthy of the blood. That was enough to prove they couldn't possibly share the grand blood of a disciple."

"……"

In other words, Ordalasse had deified his own lineage, convinced his own children would undeniably be prodigies. That meant it made perfect sense for him to think that average children were the result of infidelity, even without any damning proof.

I've got a feeling his ship is more than sinking…!

It was an irrational argument. It was only natural his vassals were bound to be distancing themselves. A seat among the Holy Elites was tempting, but when he considered how it would make him indebted to Ordalasse, Wein had some reservations, to say the least.

I mean, Steel is… Um, yeah. And Caldmellia is… Oof… Guess I'll have to team up with Gruyere…but that guy will definitely be a huge pain, too…

Wein mentally thumbed through his options again, but none of them were decent people. Well, it wasn't as if only upstanding citizens became the Holy Elites, so there wasn't much he could do with the pool of choices available to him.

Ordalasse must have taken Wein's rumination as disapproval of his own claim. He appeared sorely displeased.

"Prince Wein, it seems you do not understand the importance of blood."

"No, I'm not..."

"You have no need to be ashamed. After all, as a young man, I also focused on merit over blood when appointing vassals."

"And are you saying that was a mistake?"

"People change." Ordalasse seemed to be reminiscing. "When it comes to talent, personality, preference, ambition, it's all fluid. It can all change at any given moment. There might be vassals you expect would do great things who become deadwood half a year later."

Wein could agree about that much.

"How should a politician evaluate people? When talent and loyalty are like mirages, what about people can they believe in? The answer is blood." Ordalasse tightened his fist. "No matter who you are, you cannot cast aside your birth. The layered history of one's lineage is a foundation. Upon reflection, this is where they will always end up. In that case, there is value in trusting those who are born with the responsibility of carrying on a mighty line!"

"...I see." Wein nodded.

WHAT A DUMBASSSSSSS. He cut down Ordalasse's claim in a single stroke.

Basically, you're telling me it was a pain in the ass to choose appropriate jobs for you vassals, so you stuck to picking them based on bloodline, huh? Isn't that just admitting you're cutting corners?

For better or for worse, people did change. Even a fearless soldier would one day hope to return to his family in one piece. Even a philanthropic philosopher might drink to oblivion over unrealized dreams. Wein was on the same page for this point.

However, change itself was not a bad thing. Because people were susceptible to change, they could adapt to new situations. Once politicians acknowledged a change in a vassal, it meant nothing more than adjusting to the new circumstances and reevaluating how they should deal with the person.

If the vassal wanted money, give them money. If they wanted prestige, grant them prestige. If they missed the place of their birth, station them there. If they wanted a distraction, toss them in the red-light district.

People change. But there is one constant: They will always have desires greater than serving the nation. All you can do is offer an incentive to keep them as satisfied as possible.

This was a difficult task that had no end, of course, but Wein managed to do it. If he had time, he walked around the palace daily, observing people's expressions to confirm there were no changes in their minds and bodies. He diligently sent letters to those far away and examined any changes in their reply or brushwork. Depending on the situation, he would dispatch people or call upon them—all to confirm where their heart was at.

The fact that he knew how easily people change and tried to catch those warning signs spoke volumes about Wein's style of rule.

But Ordalasse's policy was *If it's a pain, I'm not doing it. I'll decide everything by blood.*

And that was it.

Wein couldn't stand the idea of a king double his age engaging in this behavior.

I'm gonna lay you out, he thought in a rush.

And to think that Ordalasse had even managed to create a rift with his own vassals. Wein felt nothing but disgust.

I seriously don't wanna work with this guy… What should I do?

Wein wanted to be a Holy Elite. Ordalasse's endorsement was essential for that goal. He began to seriously consider what he should do. Get Ordalasse's vote and the position, then quickly cast him aside? Cut the meeting off early and immediately realign with King Gruyere? Form ties with another Holy Elite?

"…Hmph. Seems I got heated. My apologies."

"Please, I thought nothing of it." Wein wasn't lying.

He really didn't think anything of it. In fact, he couldn't care less.

"I've always been quick to lose my cool. And these days, I haven't even been distracted by..." Ordalasse trailed off. "Come to think of it," he continued, "I forgot something. I actually had a favor I wanted to ask of you, Prince Wein."

"A favor? What might that be?" Wein gave a hollow response.

It had to involve the gold mine. But considering how he was already considering cutting ties with Ordalasse, he was hesitant to blow more money on him.

"Think you could lend me those Ashheads you're breeding in Natra?"

"——Huh?" It took Wein a few seconds to process the request.

Ashheads was the slur of choice in the West for the Flahm. Wein got that much. But what did he mean by "lend"?

"What would you need them for?"

"I was thinking of hunting them to get my mind off things. Chasing around beasts can get boring, and hunting people is an unforgivable sin. I'm nothing but grateful to our great and merciful god for providing humanoid prey for us."

"......" Wein fell into silence.

Ordalasse coughed awkwardly. "I understand your shock. You must want to say how disrespectful it is to lend god's bounty to another. But I have already hunted down all of Cavarin's Ashheads back when I was young. I haven't been able to amuse myself with a hunt in a long time. I'm guessing Natra actively breed them to prevent this, right? Smart thinking on your part."

"........."

"Oh, that's right. From what I've heard, you keep a quality Ashhead with you, right? How about we use that to go hunting together? I might be a little rusty, but I've still got faith in my skill."

From the back of the room, Zeno noticed something. Wein sat in front of her, and something inside him had changed.

Ordalasse must have sensed it, too, because he tilted his head in puzzlement.

"What's wrong, Prince Wein?"

Wein replied in a troubled tone. "Ah, nothing. I was just doing some calculations."

"Hmm?"

"Yes, but I'm finished now. Please do not worry... By the way, King Ordalasse, which would you prefer? Shall we decide now or later?"

"Hmm? For something this trivial, there's no question. We'll decide here and now."

"I see. Well, then..." Wein smiled. "Nice knowing ya, Ordalasse."

Thump! Wein bent forward over the desk—or that was what it had looked like, until he drove a kick right into Ordalasse's face.

"—Oorgah?!" Ordalasse was driven hard into the sofa, which toppled over, king and all.

Behind him, Holonyeh's eyes widened. Wein stamped over the desk and leaped out, kicking Holonyeh between the eyes and knocking him completely to the floor. Wein pivoted himself around as soon as he landed. Drawing hidden weapons from his inner pockets, he aimed for the only door connecting to outside.

"Your Majesty, that sound just now—"

The weapons pierced the foreheads of the guards who had opened the door, corpses ready to pitch out into the hallway. But Raklum came from behind and kicked them all out of the way.

"Your Highness, what happ——? Oh, I see." Surveying the inside of the room, Raklum understood in an instant. "I'll keep watch outside. But please hurry with your next move."

Raklum swiped a sword from a dead guard's corpse and tossed it to Wein.

"Yeah, I won't be long."

Sword in hand, Wein walked toward the collapsed Ordalasse, who was still writhing in agony.

"*Koff...* Wh-what're you trying to do? This is..."

Every inch of Ordalasse's face said he didn't understand the situation. Wein looked down on him coldly.

"You know, I was really torn between my options. I mean, I know this goes against every concept of manners in the world."

"What are you saying...?"

"Well, you did say we should decide now. So let's get to it." Wein prodded the king's throat with his sword.

"W-wait! I... I'm a Holy Elite...! I'm King Ordalasse, a descendant of one of Levetia's disciples...! Just what do you think that makes me?!"

"Garbage."

Without a shred of mercy or hesitation, Wein slit his throat.

Ordalasse gave a soundless cry before growing still. The metallic scent of blood filled the room.

"Zeno." Drawing the blade back, Wein turned around.

When he called out to her, Zeno jolted, shocked by the chain of events she'd just witnessed.

"U-um, Your Highness. Ah! What is going on...?!"

"Relax. There's something more important here. What will you do about him?" Wein jabbed his finger toward Holonyeh, who was still cowering in fear on the floor. "You can take him out yourself if you want."

Wein turned the hilt of the blade toward Zeno. That much was enough for Zeno to understand what he was getting at.

"W-w-w-w-w-wait! Please wait!" Holonyeh cried out, stuttering. "Please find it in your heart to forgive me! I'll never speak a word of this to anyone!"

"No," barked Wein, leaving Holonyeh at a loss for words.

But he quickly came back to himself and clung to Wein's feet.

"I—I can be useful to you, dear sir! I swear to God that I will not betray you!"

"You teamed up with Levert to try to kill me."

Holonyeh's face paled. "You... You have it all wrong! General Levert threatened me, but it was not what I wished! He was planning to make King Ordalasse retire so he could try to take control of the government! I would never willingly cooperate with him! I-I'm not lying! The plans inside my mansion prove it!"

The sword had disappeared from Wein's hand.

"Shut it, you damn traitor!"

Zeno faced Holonyeh and swung down. He dodged the blade by a hair, scrambling to escape, but he was quickly driven toward the wall. The sword was thrust right before his very nose.

"Eek...! W-wait! What is it you want?! If it's within my power, I'll give you anything...! So please, just wait...!"

"ENOUGH!" roared Zeno.

It sent a shiver down Holonyeh's spine.

"What do you mean it wasn't what you wished?! Are you saying you didn't mean to betray Marden, either?!"

"M-Marden...?" Holonyeh parroted, quivering, as if he couldn't possibly know what she was talking about. "Wh-why bring Marden up...?"

Zeno's eyes burned with rage.

As he observed her, Wein sighed. "Oh, I see. If you commit treason carelessly, it'll end up biting you in the ass. This has been a learning moment for me."

Holonyeh must have picked up a hint from Wein's words. He looked at Zeno right in front of him—shuddering with a gasp.

"A-ah... That face... You're...!"

Then the naked blade ran through him.

"—In short, I handled things with a few creative liberties."

"I see... I understand."

Wein finished speaking as he swayed along on his horse. Riding next to him, Ninym covered her eyes.

"Are you impressed?"

"I'm appalled...!" That was the natural reaction. "I can't believe it... Assassinating a Holy Elite... Of all things...!"

"Well, don't worry about it too much, Ninym. Instead of agonizing over the past, we should look forward and figure out what we're going to do from here on. Right?"

You're one to talk. Ninym almost exploded, but she kept it in.

If they hadn't been in public, she would have done him in with punches from both hands and thrown in a little knee, but now was not the time. They were surrounded by delegation members. A rowdy conversation was one thing, but it wasn't as if she could start letting fists fly in front of everyone.

I'll beat the living crap out of him when we get home, Ninym promised herself before switching gears.

She hated to admit that Wein was right, but right now, they needed to focus on safely getting home to Natra.

"Do you think we'll be followed?" Ninym asked, looking over her shoulder to observe the long road. The party had already escaped, racing toward Natra. The capital was already far behind them.

"Of course, they'll come after us. They'll find him dead after our meeting. Which makes me the obvious suspect. Plus, we immediately fled the capital, so they have no reason not to come after us.

"However," Wein added with a bright smile, "I annoyed them as much as I could before leaving. I think I bought us some time."

"What is going on?!"

The Imperial Court of Cavarin—well, more like the entire capital—had fallen into mass chaos.

The cause was King Ordalasse's death. Thinking it odd that he was a no-show to an appointed meeting, they had searched the castle and found his corpse in one of the private rooms. As soon as Levert heard the news, he got together with the other vassals and quickly imposed a gag order. It was the obvious decision. Who knew what chaos would ensue if the people discovered their king was suddenly *dead*? Not to mention, the Gathering of the Chosen for the Holy Elites was in session. And that occurred only once a year. There was no way they could let this get out.

He knew Prince Wein had been the one scheduled to meet with the king in that room. Levert quickly dispatched subordinates to apprehend him.

But despite putting the best possible plan in the worst possible circumstances into action, they were too late in dealing with Wein's parting present.

"General! The building that hosted Prince Wein is on fire!"

"What?!"

Cavarin would inevitably see Wein as the enemy. Chaos would engulf the capital. But it couldn't be further from Wein's problem. He had set the building on fire right before they made their scramble out of there.

And that wasn't all.

"General! A number of smaller fires have been confirmed in other districts of the city!"

He had given the order for all intelligence assets to vacate the city and set the hidden safe houses on fire.

"Argh…! In any case, just start putting out the fires and evacuate the citizens!"

The Festival of the Spirit was in full swing. People had gathered from all over, with more than twice the usual amount of residents currently staying in the city. Fires would cause mass panic.

"General, we have a problem!" Another subordinate came flying in.

"What now?!"

"There have been a series of unsettling rumors traveling around the castle town! As a result, a number of sporadic revolts have broken out…!"

"Rumors…?! *What* rumors?!"

The male subordinate had trouble finding the right thing to say.

"Forgive me for my words, but the rumor is that General Levert has murdered King Ordalasse, his own master…to usurp the throne…!"

Levert was lost in a stupor for a few moments before unleashing a roar.

"YOU'VE GOTTA BE KIDDING ME! WHAT THE HELL IS GOING ON?!"

"Lady Caldmellia, I have returned."

As Owl called to her from the doorway, Caldmellia continued looking out the window.

"What's the situation, Owl?"

Outside, black smoke was rising everywhere. The festival was no longer rowdy—but tumultuous. Here in the block of noble mansions, the guards of Cavarin provided tight security, but everywhere else had to be enveloped in angry bellows and violence by then.

"Right. The initial fire in Prince Wein's building has started to die down. However, news of the king's death is beginning to spread among the people. On top of that, deceptive misinformation is complicating matters, and the people are in a panic. In pockets of the city, revolts and looting have broken out."

"Wonderful." Caldmellia looked ecstatic and sighed. "He must have been bored by this little trip to do all *this*. I am nothing but thankful to Prince Wein."

"…Is this all right? It seems we are helping him."

"Do we have another choice? In addition to King Ordalasse's death, we have proof of that general's betrayal."

As Holonyeh had said in his last breath, Levert had plans to take the throne from Ordalasse. Under Wein's orders, Raklum had obtained proof from Holonyeh's mansion. As they had set fire to their building and spy hideouts to make their escape, Wein decided to do the most chaotic thing imaginable and sent the proof to Caldmellia. It was a move that said he was sure she could use that information to create even more of a mess.

And he had been exactly right.

"Now that we have this precious information, it would be a waste if we didn't use all possible means to help the fire burn bright."

Wein had seen through her meddlesome personality and quickly used it to his advantage. Both these things concerned Owl.

"…It seems the Holy Elites are all planning to evacuate the city."

"I suppose they would. They may be dumb as bricks, but at least they understand the imminent danger they're in."

"And what shall we do?"

"Please prepare our escape. After burning this place as much as possible, we will return to the land of the Holy King."

"Understood." Owl bowed and withdrew.

Caldmellia hadn't turned her eyes away from the window even once and had murmured to the boy as if he were right in front of her.

"As the one who caused this festive pandemonium, it's a shame you can't participate. But it's all too perfect. As my heartfelt thanks, I hope you'll enjoy the little trap I've laid."

"—Why don't we take a short breather?"

Raklum nodded at Wein's suggestion and relayed the announcement to the rest of the delegation. They all gave a look of relief and quickly began setting up a rest stop.

They hadn't been told of Ordalasse's death. Thinking it would only create confusion, Wein had told them they were immediately returning to Natra because he'd sensed that General Levert was plotting to attack.

"Ninym, how's our pace?"

"It's fine. It was a good idea bringing as little as possible." Ninym spread out a map. "However, the path branches off in three directions. There's the shortest one along the mountains, the central road, and an alternative route with famous sightseeing locations. Our plans had included using the central road both to Cavarin and back, but what is your opinion?"

"I heard the path along the mountain had frequent landslides."

"Yes, it is steep. Accidents happen frequently."

"Hmm... Raklum, while we're setting up to rest, send people out to check the mountain road."

"Understood." Raklum immediately began selecting who to dispatch, which Wein observed from the corner of his eye.

"Ninym, you sent a bird out to Hagal, right?"

"Yes."

"He should already be on the move, then..."

Hagal. The general protecting the gold mine.

Right after leaving the city, Ninym had sent out a messenger bird with orders to send soldiers out to meet them.

"If we can group up with Hagal, we should be able to hold off our pursuers. If it turns out the mountain road is passable, we should try to dash through it all in one go," he said.

Ninym agreed with Wein's assessment.

"By the way, Ninym, how's Zeno?"

"Depressed. Troubled. Busy."

After their escape—after dealing with Ordalasse and Holonyeh—she had fallen out of sorts. She had been wrestling with the conflicting sense of accomplishment for taking revenge on the sellout and the guilt of dirtying her own hands. Plus, she was trying to process witnessing Ordalasse's death right before her very eyes. She carried hope that Natra and the Liberation Front would form an alliance. She couldn't find common ground for all those emotions.

Ninym would have liked to speak with her and calm her mind, but they were in the middle of an emergency. She had no time to slip away.

"We have to make sure she gets back to the Remnant Army in one piece. Keep an eye on her."

Ninym nodded. "Will you join with the Remnant Army?"

"Isn't it obvious? Now that I've killed Ordalasse, we'll go to war against Cavarin even if we get out of here alive. There's no way we're getting through that without an ally—Remnant Army or not—to back us up."

"The situation keeps changing…"

"Seriously! Why did things turn out this way? —Ow, don't kick my leg."

Ninym continued to prod Wein's shin with the tip of her shoe.

"So did you decide to ally with the Remnant Army before you killed Ordalasse? Or after?"

"Before, of course. Come on, I'm not *that* reckless. I wouldn't kill him without thinking ahead."

"Hmm, I see. And I'm sure you weren't simply thinking about what your options were after killing him, right?"

"……"

"Look at me."

Wein refused to meet her eyes. Ninym sandwiched his face with both hands and forced him to look at her.

"Coming up with a plan under the assumption that you'll kill him is basically the same as thinking about it afterward…!"

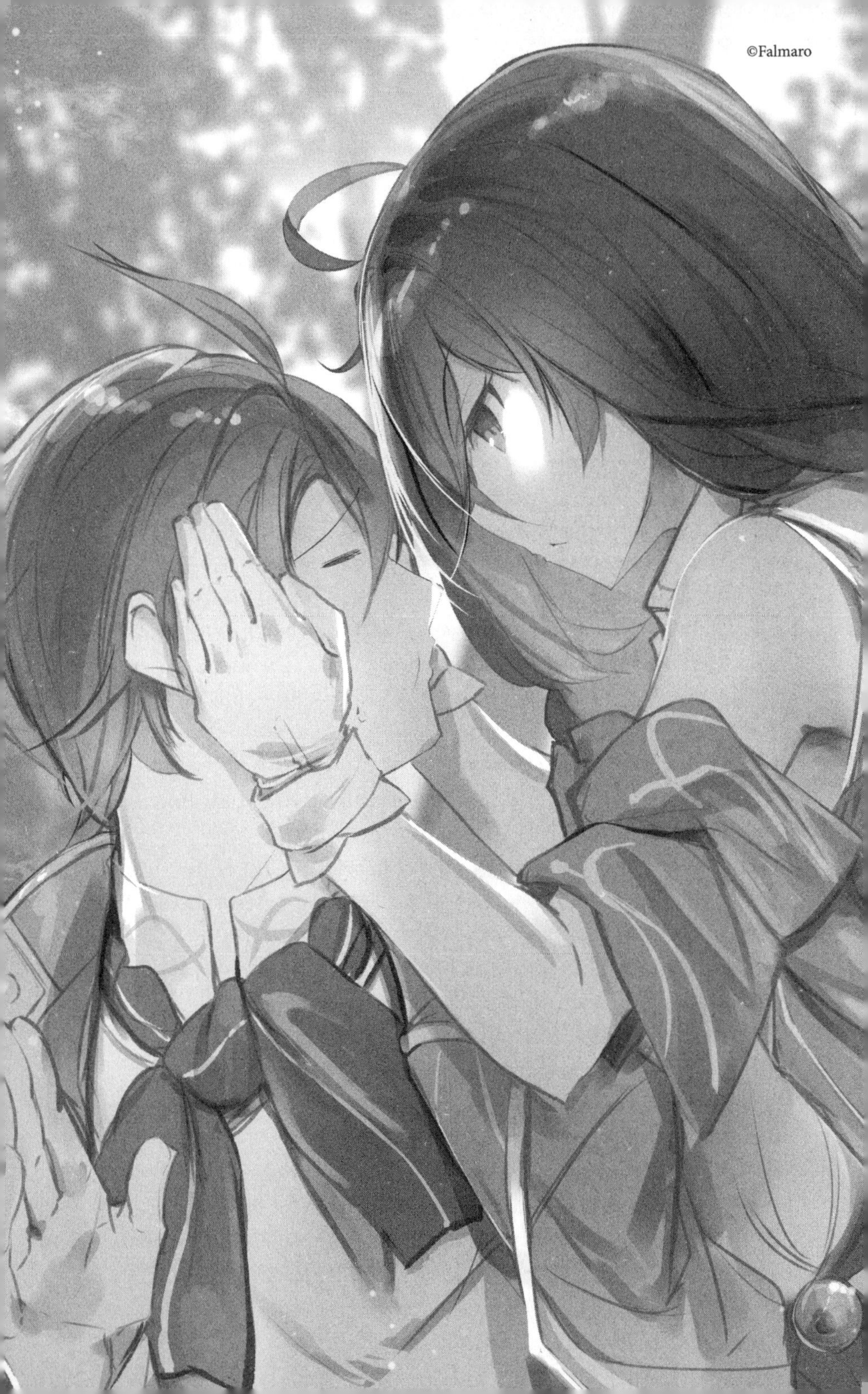

"No, well, the timing all came down to his request. If that hadn't happened, there'd be a good, decent, slight chance that the results would have been different."

"Liar! You would have killed him no matter what."

"Have some faith in my logic."

"I only believe in the situation at hand. Also, who was it that said no assassinations at the meeting?" Ninym pulled at his cheeks.

A shadow was suddenly cast over them.

As they looked up at the sky to see what was going on, they caught sight of a large bird, its wings fanned out as it came in for a landing.

"That's...word from the palace," Ninym said.

She quickly faced the bird and held out her arm, where it gently landed. A cylinder was attached to its foot, and Ninym immediately opened it to take out the scroll inside.

"What's it say, Ninym?"

Birds as clever as this one were a rare find and only used for emergencies. In other words, something at home had been urgent enough for them to dispatch it. Wein sensed a terrible premonition as Ninym faced him.

"It seems General Hagal has started a revolt."

".........Huh?"

Wein couldn't help but doubt his own ears.

Since birth, this child had been saddled with the sin of cowardice—abandoning a master to run away.

For this crime, the child was scorned daily while continuing to eke out an unfortunate existence.

When was it that this child first started to feel desire? When had this small being started to think of nothing but prestige? It didn't matter if no one understood. As someone with nothing, the child wanted an honor, even if it was only a small share of it.

That was why the teen set foot on the battlefield, fighting without pause, believing in the hope of receiving recognition one day.

And the soldier was skilled in battle, shooting through the ranks and performing brilliantly as a general. This was a time of bliss—of honor. A season golden with coins.

But then winter came.

The soldier's master raised heinous accusations, sweeping away any trace of a favorable reputation. Why? There was no answer to this question. Before long, the familiar days of scorn returned, settling back on an all-too-human body. But unlike before, seeking honor was no longer an option.

In anger, in hatred, in regret, in agony, the pariah fled home and wandered. These were days of disdain and contempt as the stigma shadowed every path.

And then finally, the wanderer arrived in a small nation to the far north. It was a poor land largely unaffected by war. It was wretched. The traveler had once led ten thousand soldiers and basked in the adulation of the people. The thought of rotting away in this country was enough to bring on a few tears.

But the king had said *A chance may come when that talent of yours will be needed. Until then, continue to hone your skills.*

The new resident believed the king's words—or wanted to believe them. Days passed without event, the hours filled with nothing except for studying and training.

It had been a year. No opportunity had come.

And then five years passed without note. But the citizen kept doubt at bay.

And then ten years of being harrowed by anxiety had gone by.

And then twenty. By now, resignation weighed heavier than lead.

And then thirty. Something in the continent had changed: the rise of a sagacious prince.

And the opportunity had finally arrived.

But reaching out hands trembling with joy, the elder noticed something… How old and wrinkled they had become—

"What troubles you, General Hagal?"

"Ngh…" General Hagal slowly opened his eyes.

They were in the defense fortress built to the west of the Jilaat gold mine. At the moment, Hagal was gathered there with a dozen of his men.

"Pardon. When I think about what my hands are about to do, they seem to slightly resist."

"I'm afraid that will not do. You are the leader of the new army of Natra, after all."

The New Army. It was the name the people gathered here had given themselves. In actuality, it was a rebel army.

It all started after Wein's delegation passed through the fortress.

Without any warning, the lords of each land led their soldiers to this fortress. They had numbered up to two thousand. The fortress's garrison had reached five hundred. Even then, their defense remained unfazed. This was primarily because the lords flew the flag of Natra and because they had Hagal. If push came to shove, they had full confidence they could expel those soldiers under their general's orders.

But in the end, no swords were crossed. Hagal explained they were the reinforcements that he had requested of the lords himself. They all deeply trusted the general, showing no trace of doubt. They let the lords' soldiers into the fortress.

No one could blame the defending soldiers. How could they have noticed that these lords were the ones who Wein had been keeping an eye on due to signs of potential mutiny?

Or that their beloved general was trying to dupe them?

The situation quickly changed. By the time the defense noticed something was off, it was already too late. The lords' forces bound them. They then took control of the mining town and declared their independence with Hagal as their leader.

"—How's the situation at the palace?"

"In an uproar, according to our spies. Well, it's not surprising since they don't have the prince there with them."

"Good. Let's really throw them into a panic."

The lords were all in high spirits as they chatted. This was only natural. They were taking a once-in-a-lifetime gamble, and right now, everything seemed to be leaning largely in their favor. Even if there were lords who didn't exactly agree, no one could put a stop to it. Wein and Ninym had been aware of this when they found out about the current situation, and the truth was, they were right.

However, three reasons brought this situation about that even the lords could have never imagined.

One, Wein had gone to Cavarin as part of the delegation. The accompanying entourage had been set to a minimum, which convinced the lords that they could easily take them out.

Two, they had Hagal on their side. He had the battle prowess to overtake Wein as head of their rebel army and was able to unite the disorderly group of rebel lords.

Three, a third party had tied the lords and Hagal together.

"—My apologies for being late," called out a woman as she entered the room.

The female merchant Ibis had been the central figure in bringing Hagal and the lords together.

"How was it, Ibis?"

"There are no issues. Prince Wein is on his way back to Natra."

The lords grew excited. Securing Wein on his return from Cavarin was a crucial step in their rebellion. As long as they had Wein, they could negotiate with either Natra or Cavarin—their choice.

"Let's get the soldiers in formation!"

"Wait, there are three roads to Cavarin. We don't know which to cover…"

"Spreading out our forces is risky."

"Then should we place them at a meeting point…?"

The lords argued over this animatedly but couldn't come to any sort of agreement. Naturally. Wein kept them far from his political administration, and the complete and honest truth was that they had no talent.

"What do you think, General Hagal?" They looked toward their leader.

The old veteran took one look at them and quietly spoke. "As mentioned, the roads leading toward us eventually converge into a single path. You should lie in wait there."

"Right, let's quickly gather our forces, and—"

"However." Hagal stopped the eager lords. "We also need to keep an eye on the soldiers originally stationed here and be prepared when Natra's main forces come to take back the fortress. Not to mention, Prince Wein's soldiers are less than one hundred. Taking along five hundred soldiers is more than enough."

They were mobilizing a quarter of their troops. The lords nodded in agreement with Hagal's logical strategy, but Ibis cut in.

"Please wait, General Hagal. Our foe is Prince Wein. I am willing to bet he can outmaneuver five hundred. To be absolutely sure, won't it be safer to dispatch a thousand more?"

"I am still concerned whether we can defend ourselves here."

"Then what if we put an end to the soldiers guarding the fortress?" Ibis cooed.

The lords shuddered. The forces here were elite soldiers who

Hagal had raised and trained himself. Even when restraining them, he'd given them strict orders not to cause any bloodshed. For fear of incurring Hagal's wrath, no one had been able to say that they should kill these soldiers to decrease the burden at the fortress.

But surprisingly enough, Hagal gave an indifferent reply devoid of any emotion.

"They may still be loyal to Natra now, but I know they'll change their minds to follow me if Wein dies. Then we'll have soldiers with battle experience. It would be a waste to get rid of them here."

"...I see; you're right. Well, what if we take half of our soldiers to the front lines? You may be concerned over insufficient forces, General Hagal, but please do not worry. I said so before, but reinforcements are headed this way."

It was the lords who expressed joy at this—not Hagal.

"Oh. How heartening!"

"I knew it! We weren't the only ones fed up with Prince Wein."

"Of course not. What kind of chump puts Flahm in positions of power? And why would he ever be popular?"

Hagal looked at the excited nobles from the corner of his eye, then stared at Ibis.

"There's no question that more forces are on their way, right, Ibis?"

"Of course."

"...Very well. We'll blockade the main road with a thousand soldiers and lie in wait for Wein. Prepare to move out."

""Right!""

The lords all stood up and left the room to carry out Hagal's orders. Hagal stayed in his place and finally looked at Ibis, who had lagged behind.

"Ibis, once everything is over—"

"I know. As promised, I shall return to your homeland, restore your honor, and arrange for you to be received as a general. I'm certain it will be a simple matter for my master."

"Very well…"

"Everything has gone favorably because of Your Excellency… Reaching out to you was worthwhile, as were the others."

"Are you being sarcastic?"

"I'm being honest. I'm sure you have your own opinions about the prince."

This was neither a question nor a jest, and Hagal remained silent a long while, then spoke as if to himself.

"…I am old. I cannot return to that time of my life in Natra. Forgive me, Prince Wein. Everything is already too late."

Meanwhile, Wein was troubled.

Okaaay. What to do?

Choosing to trust a piece of information lay largely on the deliverer's authority and their relationship to the receiving party. People tended to believe information that came from a person in power, a specialist, or an acquaintance.

As for why, it was because there were time and physical constraints.

Take, for example, a strange animal scratching at the house next door. You could decide to check it out yourself, of course. But when it came down to foreign affairs, it wasn't so easy to pop over and see things for yourself.

If a stranger insisted it was a red bird, and a friend—or an influential figure—claimed it had blue plumes, most would generally believe the latter.

In other words…

"Ninym, do you think Hagal is a traitor?"

"All signs would normally point to fake news."

They had come down to this question.

General Hagal. He had rank, skill, and a long record of

accomplishments in service to Natra. Even if the dispatcher had used the bird reserved for emergencies, Ninym—much less the citizens of Natra—couldn't help but think there was some sort of mistake to suspect him of betraying their country.

—However, there was one more factor when it came to how much information could be trusted.

"This might mean that last scheme of yours drained him of all affection he had for you."

"*NYAAAAAGH!*" Wein yelped.

By that last scheme, she meant the plan to use Hagal as bait to draw out any dissenters. Hagal and Wein had intentionally spread rumors for this purpose, but no one could deny Hagal's loss of reputation might have left him inclined to follow through with this scheme.

While the timing had been unexpected, Wein had hoped Hagal would gather a group of rebels, so it was realistic to believe he was raising an army.

Could he pinpoint a specific cause for this information? That would drastically change the information's believability.

"I've said many times that I was opposed to it."

"I know! I know, okay? I get it! I was wrong! Hagal's betrayal! Cavarin coming after us! It's aaaaaaall my fault!"

"Wow, you're so right… I'm shocked…"

"Seriously. I mean, even *I* think I'm a piece of garbage…"

They could reflect on it all they wanted once they got out of this situation.

"The first issue is whether there is a rebel army and whether Hagal is the mastermind. Then, there's the question of whether he actually betrayed us or if he's under circumstances that give him no choice but to obey…"

"Since we're short on time, we should assume the worst. Assume there is a rebel army, that Hagal is their leader, that he betrayed us by his own will. Let's put his motive aside and operate under those conditions."

Wein nodded at her assessment. "The three roads ahead are different lengths, but once you pass through them, they merge into one. I imagine Hagal is waiting for me there to either capture or kill me."

"According to reports, it seems Hagal has already gathered soldiers. He'll be moving quickly. Even if we use the mountain path as originally planned, it will be difficult to pass through before they cut us off."

"But our options outside of that are kinda meh…"

Wein had heard the rebel army numbered close to two thousand. He had no idea how many were coming for them, but it'd probably be in the five hundred to one thousand range. And if Hagal was the one giving the orders, it would be hard to fight or escape if he got pinned down even once.

That said, if they ventured off the main road and got bogged down, Cavarin would catch up from behind. They had investigated the troops in the capital of Cavarin ahead of time: Pursuit would likely comprise mostly horsemen and anywhere between two to five hundred soldiers. Meaning another enemy that Wein's group couldn't handle.

Honestly, things weren't looking good. As they wondered what to do, Raklum rushed up to them.

"Your Highness, those who went to investigate the mountain path have returned."

"Oh, how'd it go?"

Raklum shook his head. "I have unfortunate news. There was a landslide the other day, and now it seems the road is impassable."

Ninym moaned at this, unbidden. They were in dire straits, and yet, they couldn't use the shortest road. It made their chances of getting past Hagal's blockade all the slimmer.

"…And how long will it take to clear?" Wein asked.

"The shortest time frame is ten days."

Ten days. It would be impossible to wait that long. Ninym was certain Cavarin would catch up by then.

Options, options. We can either pray for the safety of Wein and his select few as they attempt to race through the central highway on horseback before the rebel army arrives or leave the main roads and proceed cautiously in the hopes of avoiding discovery.

Either one had a considerable risk. Wasn't there a more reliable option that could at least help Wein out of this situation?

As Ninym thought about this, she gave Wein a sidelong glance and noticed that a bold smile was breaking out on his lips.

"—Let's get moving, Raklum. Break's over. Get everyone ready to go."

"Understood!" Raklum left quickly to do as he was instructed.

"Ninym, call Zeno over. We've got some things to discuss."

"Understood... But what are you going to do, Wein?"

Ninym couldn't help but ask, and Wein replied mischievously.

"Put their unseen backs to good use."

A few days had passed since Wein's group escaped from Cavarin. Levert had finally started to subdue the capital and ordered an adjutant to send out a pursuit party.

"Listen up! Capture the prince of Natra at any cost! He assassinated King Ordalasse!"

Though he faced his subordinates with fervor, Levert was still having a tough time dealing with internal affairs. After King Ordalasse's sudden passing, Levert had become the core of the provisional government. As a general, he had been initially entrusted with military matters, and he'd also been the one issuing orders to quell the capital, so it only made sense for him to fill the position.

But the rumors that he had murdered his own master made it seem as if he had been scheming to gain the position in the ensuing chaos of the king's death. Levert was well aware of this.

To make things worse, the Holy Elites had returned to their home countries. If they had either declared their confidence in the new provisional government or appointed a crown prince as a new Holy Elite, he would have probably been able to stop the situation from deteriorating.

But the reality was that he was currently plagued with scandal and left facing nothing but protests. Things were not looking to be in his favor. The citizens had not only lost their king but also a huge structural support system—the Holy Elites. Of course, the citizens—and even the government officials—would be consumed by panic. The lords of the realm must have started to seriously weigh their choices. They needed a scapegoat or an easy reason to explain it all. That was why Levert was in a very precarious position indeed.

"We must catch that prince and expose him as the mastermind…!"

In truth, Levert had one more option. He could foist the blame on any old person and wrap things up that way—but he wouldn't take that route out.

Because rage consumed Levert—for the blow to his pride that this uproar had caused and for the king's death. He needed justification for invading Natra. That had driven Levert to take action.

"Come on, get going! We can still catch them!"

Levert's close aide, Kustavi, led his subordinates as they raced down the northern road—all cavalry, coming in at around five hundred strong. It was almost excessive, since their opponent's party exceeded no more than fifty. Levert had been faced with some criticism for sending out soldiers en masse—for the turmoil in the capital had yet to die down—but he silenced them. He couldn't allow them get away, even if it was only a one-in-a-million chance.

"Captain, the scouts have returned!"

A few horsemen raced toward Kustavi, confirming the condition of the road ahead.

"How is it? Did you find out which road they took?"

"Yes! There were signs of them on the central road. We found discarded luggage."

Kustavi raised a brow. "They didn't take the mountain road?"

They must have known they were being followed. The delegation should have taken the shortest road, risking its dangers. And yet—

"Apparently, there had been a landslide before their group could reach the road. It's still being cleaned up. It's currently impossible to pass," explained one of his subordinates.

That made sense to Kustavi. He knew that road was basically falling apart. God had to be punishing Wein for his wickedness. Levert was chuckling to himself when he suddenly became suspicious of something else.

"Captain, let us set off in pursuit. We should be able to overtake them," urged the subordinate.

But Kustavi shook his head, eyes glinting. "No. We should hold off. This must be a setup."

"A setup?"

"Yes..."

Kustavi had instinctively reached down to touch his foot, where Wein had pierced him with a spear. After all, he had been the one who led the attack against the delegation.

With his own two eyes, Kustavi had witnessed the prince make his way out of his predicament, weaponizing the resources available to him and exercising his snap judgment. That was why Kustavi wasn't convinced that he'd leave behind obvious tracks.

"I'm guessing they're planning on taking a detour—and trying to trick us into thinking they took the central road. That way they wouldn't be pursued from behind," he reasoned.

The subordinates all seemed to understand. It really was a cheeky little trick. But now that they had seen through the ruse, it was clear Wein's group had specifically chosen the longest route to Natra.

"Come on! They'll be at the end of the byway!" barked Kustavi, and the party in pursuit quickly set off.

"We've successfully deployed the troops, General Hagal."

"Mm-hmm."

Three roads to Cavarin. Led by Hagal, the rebel army of a thousand soldiers took up positions at the crossroad.

"Even the prince won't be able to escape this one," boasted one of the lords near him.

The others nodded in agreement.

That was when a woman cut into their conversation. "...But will this be okay?"

It was Ibis. She had accompanied them to the battlefield. The lords were in a foul mood because she was a woman—and a lowly merchant at that! And she hadn't simply followed them to the battlegrounds; she was acting like she owned the place! But there was no denying that she played a huge part in helping them rise to action, so they said nothing.

"To prepare, we should give the right to command all the forces to General Hagal."

Like she implied, the rebel forces were not unified—because the lords had each brought their own soldiers.

Many of the lords had come here with the intention of commanding their own armies. It just wouldn't sit right with them if Hagal led their personal soldiers to their deaths.

And what's more, Hagal himself didn't act as if he wished for that, either.

"I know I am the symbolic head, but I share their opinion... And with this many soldiers, I don't think we'll have any difficulty capturing the prince, even under different commands."

"What the general says."

"Women should stay back and keep their mouths shut!"

With this much pushback, Ibis couldn't say anything more. And thus, the hodgepodge army remained divided. They continued to lie in wait for the prince.

"—Hmm." Hagal caught the sound of horses' hooves.

It wasn't from one horse—or two, or ten, or even twenty.

It had to be over a hundred cavalrymen coming their way!

"The enemy is coming! Ready your weapons!"

As Hagal raised his voice, the lords and soldiers scattered into their positions. As they did, the sound grew closer—and five hundred horsemen appeared before them.

With the scene before him, Kustavi quickly called out, "Halt! All forces, at ease!"

At their captain's order, the horsemen slowed and came to a stop. After craning his neck to look at their situation, Kustavi looked forward once again. There were around a thousand soldiers ready for battle on the road ahead.

"Who the hell are they…?" He groaned—visibly confused and on guard.

Things had been going great until he had come up with his theory that the main road was a trap and raced toward the byway. But they had gone on and on without encountering even a shadow of the delegation. Kustavi was starting to get impatient. He wondered if he had read into the situation too deeply.

But it wasn't as if he could just call it quits. He had believed the delegation was on the road ahead and continued onward— Now, they were face-to-face with a mysterious army.

"They don't fly the flag of Natra. And they're all in different uniforms. Could they be bandits?"

"Would bandits be in formation? What kind of army is this…?"

It was an odd situation. They weren't the only ones disoriented, either; he could feel the confusion radiating from the other army. In other words, neither knew the identity of the other.

Kustavi asked himself what they should do. How should they deal with this unexpected encounter?

As he stressed over this, a single horseman cautiously approached them.

This was their chance. His only target was the prince of Natra. He wanted to avoid any meaningless battles. Kustavi got ready to send out a soldier in response, and—

"The enemy is attacking!" shrieked someone from behind.

What's with this person?

That question had been occupying Zeno's mind ever since they'd hightailed it out of Cavarin. She had known he'd had the skills to drive back Marden, and from their conversations on the road to Cavarin, she knew his values were quiet yet resolute. But now, she was stupefied—by his method of undermining enemy nations with books, his peculiar way of thinking that could rival the Holy Elites, and his decisiveness in murdering King Ordalasse.

As they'd approached the three forked roads at last, the enemy had closed in on them from both sides.

"We'll let the party in pursuit pass us," he had said, "then go head-to-head with Hagal's rebel army."

She'd been dumbfounded. That would be the last thing that she would ever think to do.

"More specifically, we'll let our pursuers pass us and then attack them from behind—right as the two sides confront each other. Then, we'll break through the chaos and turn the whole thing into a chaotic battlefield."

When Wein put it that way, it felt as though this was the only option. That, of course, meant they needed a way to let the party in pursuit pass them, but—

"That's simple," Wein had commented. "We can leave our luggage and belongings on the main road to signal we were there, then hide on the mountain road until they pass us."

The mountain road was prone to landslides, providing plenty of shelter under rocks. It wouldn't be difficult to hide fifty people. And since the party in pursuit wanted to catch up to Wein's group as quickly as possible, their investigation into their whereabouts would be perfunctory at best.

Wein would win, no matter what course his pursuers chose: They would either run down the central road upon spotting their luggage—or try to read into his next steps and take the byway. They couldn't take the mountain pass, since there was that recent landslide, which left only two options. At least, making them think they only had two options would ensure Wein's success.

But could they really pull it off?

Logically? Yes. But it was only a theory. If the party in pursuit had been more thorough in their investigations, the delegation would have been caught in a fight with no way to retreat. If that happened, Wein would be captured—and the rest killed.

And yet, Wein decided to put this theory to the test. He had come to terms with the possibility of death and pushed it aside as if it was the most natural thing in the world.

Is that what you call the makings of a king?

She had no idea, though there was one thing she could say for sure.

The unguarded backs of the party in pursuit before them was proof his plan had succeeded.

The series of events that followed would be best described as a chain reaction.

"Wh-what?! What's going on?!"

The surprise attack from behind threw the pursuers into absolute chaos. Even though the possibility of being struck from behind was psychologically tormenting, the cavalrymen couldn't easily turn around as such a maneuver would entail deftly maneuvering their horses. Unfortunately, their comrades to the left and right would get in the way and prevent them from moving freely.

This meant the only way out was forward. The horsemen could put some distance between them and fix the situation—but if they moved ahead any farther, they'd only be faced with the rebel army ready to confront them.

"C-calm down! Under no circumstances are you to attack!"

"Don't retreat! If you do, I'll have your head!"

"Dammit! Who are they?! Are they the enemy...?!"

Five hundred horsemen had come into sight. That alone had been enough for the lords to fall into chaos. Trying to organize the soldiers in this state was virtually impossible. They hurled contradicting orders at their troops, and the soldiers' organization completely dissolved.

But to the pursuers, it looked exactly like they were preparing for attack by breaking out from their initial formations.

Which was how the two parties somehow landed on the same page.

"All right, it looks like it's come to this. Charge! Break through the forward lines!"

"The enemy is attacking! All units, prepare to engage!"

And so, the battle between a thousand rebels and five hundred horsemen began.

The battlefield had turned into a melee.

The pursuers rushed forward and failed to break through the defenses of the rebel army. But they managed to land a huge blow. Friend and foe jumbled together as they crossed swords.

Agh, I've had enough! Who would have thought it would turn out like this...?!

Out in the middle of the madness and surrounded by guards, Ibis clicked her tongue. She had planned to kill Wein here after he escaped from Cavarin. The prince was dangerous. If left alive, she was sure he would become an enemy of her master, Caldmellia.

But she hadn't found Wein—all she had caught was a mysterious band of cavalry.

Just before she realized they must have been the pursuers sent from Cavarin and that they could try to make peaceful contact, the battle had begun.

Why would the party in pursuit show up before the prince...?!

Where in the world *was* the prince? Could the pursuing party from Cavarin seriously have overlooked him on the road? She could have probably figured it out if the rebels and the pursuers could just talk, but chaos had broken out, and that chance was now long gone.

...No, wait. This mess couldn't possibly be...

Ibis realized something, snapping up her head to look out over the battlefield.

"...I see. You've certainly outdone yourself."

Ibis quickly began to move. Taking the guards with her, she headed to the heart of the rebel army where Hagal and the lords were barking out orders. The mishmash of an army hadn't yet completely collapsed because several of Hagal's forces were issuing orders on his behalf and helping hold things together by a thin thread.

"General Hagal!"

"…Ah, Ibis. What is it?"

"This is all a trap set by Prince Wein! He's having us clash with that cavalry so he can slip through in the chaos! I imagine he is aiming to release the guards from the fortress!" she shouted.

The lords became more confused and at a total loss for words.

Among all this, Hagal looked around calmly. "We'll gather any soldiers we can and chase the prince. Order the rest to fall back. Even their cavalry is unlikely to pursue us needlessly."

""U-understood!""

Coordinating with nearby lords, Hagal swiftly gathered soldiers—around two hundred in number. The group withdrew from the battlefield and headed east toward the fortress at full speed.

There are fifty people in the prince's delegation. They must have split off into small groups to slip by more easily, which means there must be a group or two that won't make it to the other side. His delegation must have gotten smaller—and exhausted from escaping Cavarin.

At this rate, we can definitely catch them, Ibis thought assuredly as she traveled with Hagal.

Her conviction soon became reality. Sensing movement, they caught members of Wein's group as they made their way through the wilderness. It had been less than twenty people. As expected, two hundred soldiers would be more than enough to bring them down once they caught them.

When Wein realized he'd been discovered, he did the unexpected. Rather than trying to escape, he stopped and looked behind him.

Hagal's forces got close enough that both parties could hear each other and stopped.

There were two hundred soldiers in high spirits and twenty

exhausted men. It was obvious what would happen if the two sides crossed swords.

But even now, Wein refused to fall apart.

"General Hagal. Glad to see you're doing well." Wein greeted him as if they were meeting in the royal court.

His nonchalance—which lacked any animosity or threat—was what had sparked fear.

"...Are you not even going to ask for a reason?" Hagal asked.

Wein smiled. "I'll ask after I win."

There was no way a single rebel could possibly know that this place had been where Levert's assassins had ambushed Wein's party on their way to Cavarin.

"—Now, attack!"

The Remnant Army of Marden emerged from the shadows of the boulders and attacked Hagal's rebel army.

"Well, then," said Wein to Zeno before they hid themselves away on the mountain path.

"The plan is to slip in and out of the battlefield right after they start engaging with the pursuers, and everything turns crazy. But Hagal or someone else is bound to catch on to us. Which is why," Wein continued, "we're going to use that to lure in our pursuers, bring them down, and weaken their fighting power."

"...Isn't this when we should be thinking of an escape route instead?" Zeno pointed out.

Wein shook his head. "If possible, this is the point where I want to either capture Hagal or reduce the lords' troops. We might be facing Cavarin in a single battle after this, and I want to conserve as much time and manpower as possible. Out there, they're getting riled up over the Cavarin—who they wouldn't even shed a single tear over if the entire cavalry was annihilated. I gotta take advantage of that, no matter what."

Ninym raised a hand. "If you're the decoy, where will we get the forces to bring them down?"

"The Remnant Army of Marden is going to help us out."

"Huh?" Zeno couldn't stop herself.

"In exchange, we're offering a joint front against Cavarin and assistance to revive the royal capital of Marden. What do you say, Zeno?"

"U-umm, well, I can't really make that decision on my own…"

"I'm pretty sure *you can*."

Wein's assertion left Zeno completely speechless. Their eyes locked for a moment.

Finally, Zeno spoke as if in resignation. "…I will send a bird out with orders to have soldiers hide in the appointed location. However, Your Highness, I cannot guarantee they will actually be waiting for us until we get there."

Wein chuckled. "Trust only has value because there's the potential of betrayal. Isn't that right?"

Three hundred soldiers from Marden were lying in wait. They were just strong enough to bring down the rebel forces that came after Wein.

Furthermore, the rebels had been slapped together to make an army. The surprise attack simply crushed their already flagging morale; most were already surrendering or escaping. The rest of the soldiers' resistance gradually weakened until finally they all dropped their weapons. One lone veteran general stood in the center, his grip tightening over his sword—Hagal.

"…Well done, Your Highness," he said, standing before Wein. "These old bones are no match for you."

From atop his horse, Wein called out to him. "Don't you have any words to defend yourself?"

"I do not. However, this was entirely my own decision. The fortress guards had no part in it."

"...You'll be put on trial. The punishment will fit the crime."

"I have no regrets. After all, I did all this because I thought it was necessary."

And with that, Hagal tossed his weapon to the ground.

He was quickly restrained, and Wein's party immediately went to infiltrate the fortress occupied by the rebel army. They already had a full understanding of its layout, of course, so releasing the guards who'd been placed under house arrest was not difficult.

They carried out a ferocious assault and expelled the rebels in short order.

Meanwhile, the pursuers retreated, and once the few hundred returning rebels found out they lost the fortress and that Hagal had been apprehended, they quickly surrendered as well. The battlefield was quiet once more.

And thus, Hagal's rebellion came to an end.

"...Honestly, I can't believe things turned out this way."

Gazing at the liberated fortress from far off, Ibis clicked her tongue. After Marden's surprise attack, she had realized there was no chance of victory and escaped as fast as she could.

"We could have never imagined that general would be so useless."

Forming this plan had cost a hefty sum of money and a decent amount of time—from contacting and secretly supporting the lords dissatisfied with Wein to deciding the right timing for enacting the plan altogether. And yet, Wein was fine, and the rebellion was destroyed.

But there were advantages to failure.

"Hagal will now be gone from the stage," her subordinate stated matter-of-factly.

Ibis nodded reluctantly. Wein had been the plan's main target, but the next best thing—Hagal—was someone who they had wanted either killed or expelled from society. After all, the military strength of Natra would fall drastically without him.

"As the ringleader of the revolt, he can't escape execution... Let us enjoy witnessing how the war with Cavarin unfolds from here on," Ibis spat like venom.

Then, she turned on her heel and walked away.

Just as she'd said, news of Hagal's execution spread across the nation soon after.

General Hagal's unexpected revolt came as a huge shock to the citizens of Natra.

Why would someone who had trusted and faithfully served the royal family act in this way? This was on everyone's minds, and all sorts of rumors and speculation ran rampant.

But no one could agree on a conclusion. That was because Hagal the ringleader had not given a single word of protest.

Even those trying to decide if he deserved clemency were having trouble coming up with a defense. Raising a sword against your master was a sin. If he had propped up his accomplishments as a justifiable reason to spare him, he might have been able to avoid execution. But it seemed that Hagal did not have the desire to go through with that.

If he had no desire to save himself, no one could change that. The court declared Hagal guilty, and he was sentenced to death. He was beheaded within the day. Most of the lords and others who had participated in the revolt were executed, too.

Though it had been a necessity, the military troops of Natra had lost a core member, causing anxiety to rise in the nation. But that fear was wiped out in the most surprising way.

Of all things, it was Cavarin's ridiculous proclamation that Wein had killed their recently departed King Ordalasse.

"What an insult to our crown prince!"

"I heard some guy named Levert has taken over, and he's the one who killed the king."

"They're just making up a reason to go to war…!"

"Using General Hagal's death as an opportunity? They're a bunch of beasts that just look human."

In this way, the citizens' fear quickly changed to rage toward Cavarin. The reaction must have been partially motivated by their innate desire to shake off their fears.

In any case, with talk of the looming war with Cavarin on the horizon and expectations for Wein to defeat them, it wasn't long before people no longer spoke of Hagal's death—

Back to the present.

With his people's hope all on him, Wein was at the base of the Remnant Army of Marden.

There was but one reason: to form an official alliance against Cavarin.

"I wonder what they'll bring to the table?" Ninym asked Wein as they waited on standby in the room. "Everything is going their way, right?"

"I'd say so. An unfortunate misunderstanding has left the relationship between Natra and Cavarin volatile, and we've agreed to support each other as a united force on the battlefield as long as they act as reinforcements. The Marden side couldn't ask for a better outcome."

"An 'unfortunate misunderstanding.'"

"You know, this whole thing pains me, too."

"That's not the impression I get."

"Well, these things happen." Wein shrugged.

"By the way, I know we involved the Remnant Army to suppress the rebels, but wasn't there a possibility that they would betray us?"

Wein shouldered the sin of killing a king. The Remnant Army had the option of capturing him and using him in diplomatic negotiations with Cavarin.

But Wein shook his head. "That'd be tricky. First of all, there is no way the Remnant Army would want to join up with Cavarin from an emotional standpoint. Even from an economic perspective, we're not sure when Levert's regime will collapse, and even if they somehow make a deal, Cavarin might skip out on the bill in the end. Plus, more than anything else, I was by Zeno's side all throughout the battle."

Just as he finished his sentence, the door swung open. Jiva appeared.

"Prince Regent. We are prepared for the meeting."

"Got it. Let's go, Ninym."

Wein and Ninym left the room and continued down the hallway. Jiva talked as he guided them.

"By the way, Your Highness, I heard you took very good care of Zeno."

"Of course. She was an important traveling companion."

"Thank you very much. I was surprised when the message came, requesting we hide our army." Jiva offered a wry smile as they arrived in front of their destination. "Prince Helmut is waiting for you. Please come inside."

Jiva opened the door. Accompanied by Ninym, Wein followed him inside.

Wein saw the person waiting for him. His eyes widened slightly, and he gave a small smile.

"Might I ask your name once more, Prince Helmut?"

"Zenovia."

Zeno—Zenovia— placed her hand on her chest as she answered.

"I am the Kingdom of Marden's eldest princess, Zenovia Marden. I'm pleased to make your acquaintance, Prince Wein."

*   *   *

"You're not very surprised," noted Zenovia, smiling as she sat across from Wein. "I gather that you noticed?"

"No, you definitely got me."

Unlike when they were traveling together, there was no question she was a girl. He had known from the very beginning that she was disguised as a boy, but now that she was dressed differently, he could hardly recognize her.

Especially with those big breasts. Wein couldn't hide his surprise at how she'd managed to tuck them away.

"—Hey." Ninym stabbed the back of Wein's head with her pen. *Be serious*, she seemed to say. Wein rubbed his head.

"I realized that you, Zeno—I mean, Princess Zenovia—were one of the royal family while we were in Cavarin. However, I was only half sure that Prince Helmut and you were the same person."

"You were half sure? And what made you realize for sure?"

"Your response when I requested reinforcements."

"…I see, so that was your objective. It seems as if you can solve any mystery through even the most trivial conversation, Prince."

Zenovia smiled wryly, and Wein responded in turn.

"I have a question as well. Was your Prince Helmut charade an attempt to raise the soldiers' morale?"

"You're right," Zenovia admitted with a nod. "When Cavarin attacked the capital, I was able to escape thanks to our most loyal retainer, Jiva. I then decided to form an army in order to take back the capital, but as you can see, I am a woman."

Whether she was royalty or not, she was still a woman. In a country that was as heavily influenced by the Teachings of Levetia as Marden, it was no surprise she didn't have the status required to answer that calling.

"However, the other royals had all been executed, and there was no

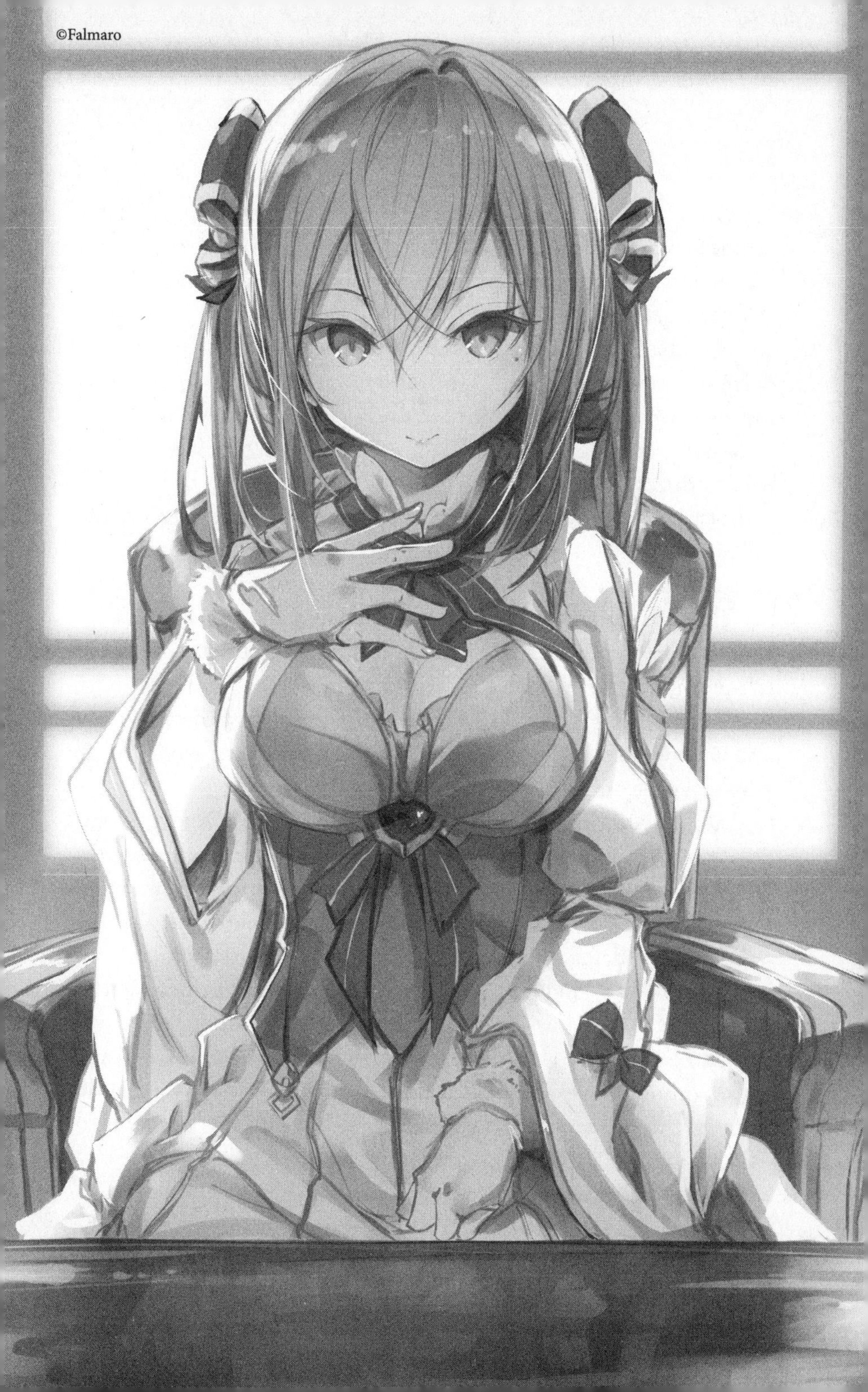

one else to take the position. When Prince Helmut was put to death, no one had been able to tell it was him. Which was why I took his name, put on a helmet and armor, and pretended to be him around the clock."

"But wasn't that inconvenient for you?"

"Not at all. The armor was so light that even I could wear it. Furthermore, the fact that only a select few vassals knew my face was my saving grace, so I was able to live on as Jiva's nephew Zeno."

What did it mean for her vassals to not know the face of their eldest princess?

In the back, Ninym murmured. "The eldest princess hardly made public appearances, rarely seen due to her poor health. There was even a rumor that she had passed away."

"That was indeed a rumor. As you can see, I am in fine health."

It was here that Zenovia seemed to laugh at herself with some self-derision.

"The truth is, Father…His Majesty…had admonished me harshly and had me cloistered in the imperial villa. Ironically enough, that is why I was the only one able to escape."

I see, Wein thought. He knew well the love she had for her country. It wasn't hard to imagine that her father would send away his loudmouthed daughter who refused to silence her righteous indignation over his corrupt reign. It was a perfectly likely story.

As he considered this, Zenovia turned to the matter at hand.

"Prince Wein, might I turn our meeting toward a discussion of an alliance?"

"Of course, that was my intention. I have no plans to null my earlier promise. We will fight against Cavarin with the Liberation Front to free the capital of Marden."

"…"

"Is something not sitting well with you?"

"To be perfectly honest, I am unsure whether to continue the fight with Cavarin."

Not only Wein and Ninym but also Jiva beside them looked surprised.

The princess went on. "I thought that if I could just go to the capital of Cavarin and meet the Holy Elites, we might have a chance. That I would gain their support if I could only bring our distress and Cavarin's barbarism to their attention. But I was much too naive. I was as concerned as I could be about my nation, but I had none of the skill required to lead it."

Zenovia thought of the Holy Elites she met in Cavarin's capital. Each one of them was full of will. And right in front of her, she felt it coming from Wein, too.

"How can I take back Marden's capital and revive the nation? How can I contend with people like you? Even if I pretended to be Helmut at the outset, I don't know how long I can keep up that charade."

"…"

"What if the efforts of the Liberation Front only hurt the citizens unnecessarily…? That is my greatest fear." Zenovia then smiled. It was somewhat pained. "What do you think, Prince Wein? Can you persuade someone like me?"

All eyes in the room fell on Wein. He was silent for a moment as he thought it over.

"Zeno." Wein had intentionally called her by this name. "First, you should fix that arrogant attitude."

"What?" Zenovia blinked in surprise. "Y-you think I'm arrogant…?"

"Protecting the powerless citizens alone? Guiding them? That's arrogance if I ever saw it. If you ask me, the citizens can live fine on their own without a king or whatever."

Everyone in the room looked taken aback. Wein faced them all and expanded on his theory.

"Don't look down on your people, Zeno. Authority is an illusion, and every last citizen has the willpower and ability to kill a king. That's why kings rule with a cautious hand, and their subjects continue to observe whether that king is bringing them any benefit. It's not a one-way road. There has to be mutual benefit to build what we call a country."

"..."

"That's why, Zeno, you should use the people as much as possible to achieve your own goals. After all, the people are going to wring you dry in pursuit of theirs. I'll say it so there's no mistake: The true nature of the relationship between a king and his subjects is nothing more than fellow accomplices."

Wein finished and looked at Zeno. His eyes seemed to be asking *So what are you going to do?*

"...Can I really wish for that? To take back Marden? To release it from Cavarin's grasp?"

"Naturally," Wein said. "Get your people to buy in and take back Marden together. You can worry about the government and everything else once that's been taken care of. Even if you don't have the skill now, people can change. Even if you fail, you'll either die or be singled out for criticism. And there isn't much of a difference between the two. There's no point in worrying over a miscalculation."

"...I'm certain you are the only one on the continent who can call that a miscalculation, Prince Wein." Zeno smiled wryly. Unlike before, she seemed more relaxed. "Thank you. You have washed all my fears away. I shall face Cavarin all for the sake of my wish."

"Sounds like a plan... Well then, in that case, let's resolve one more issue, Princess Zenovia. It concerns your Helmut disguise."

"Do you have a plan of some sort?"

"Of course. It's actually simple. —Right, Prince Helmut?"

Huh? Zenovia looked confused.

Wein grinned.

"I understand your concern. Once you face off against Cavarin, there will always be a slim chance that something may happen. But even if you fail, you still have Princess Zenovia to entrust into our nation's care," waxed Wein, as if acting in a play.

Zenovia shivered. After all, she understood his intentions.

"If that time does come, I will do my best to put Princess Zenovia on the throne. There will be some opposition to a ruling queen, but with my nation's support, it will be done."

"Prince Wein, you…"

Prince Helmut would officially die in the next battle against Cavarin. According to the story, Zenovia, who had been entrusted in Natra's care, would rise as Marden's true successor. This would release her from her Helmut guise.

If she went along with this plan, the cooperation of Natra would be essential in her ascension to the throne, and it would likely be difficult to defy their wishes from here on out.

"What? There's nothing to worry about. —We're friends, right?" Wein chided Zenovia, who had become more timid.

Then he switched completely and proceeded with negotiations over his own national interests. Even after they repelled Cavarin, and the Kingdom of Marden was revived once more, he was sure to take advantage of their political instability.

Zenovia didn't think he was being vague or evasive. Rather, she had a feeling that she understood his character. This prince named Wein was kind and treated everyone equally in every circumstance.

"…Prince Wein, may I bring up one more final matter?"

"Name it."

"Earlier, you called the Holy Elite a bunch of shams, but you're truly no better."

Wein shrugged. "I'll take that as a compliment."

And thus, the conference resulted in an alliance between Natra and the Remnant Army of Marden.

A month later, the war between Cavarin and their Allied Forces would begin.

Tholituke. The former royal capital of Marden.

The Allied Forces moved out to surround the city under Cavarin occupation. By entering this war, they claimed it was their moral duty to release Tholituke from Cavarin's unjust rule.

The Allied Forces were an army of about seven thousand, comprised of four thousand from Natra and the rest from the Remnant Army. The soldiers of Natra had been capped by their monetary revenue from the mine, paying however many they could afford and gathering as many guards as possible. The Remnant Army used their remaining fortune to mobilize everything they could muster.

In response to this, the guards stationed in Cavarin chose to tightly bar the gates and hole up in the castle. This bought them time as they waited for their homeland to send reinforcements.

"Everything's going just as planned," Wein noted in the tent of their temporary command center. "Let's strictly forbid all troops from carrying out any excessive attacks, especially inside the castle. Instead, we'll continue to emphasize that we are the Liberation Front led by Marden's true successor, Prince Helmut, and that our goal is to save the royal capital."

"Understood."

As Wein's subordinates were dispatched, Zeno began to speak up, sitting next to Wein and dressed in armor as Prince Helmut.

"Psychological warfare, huh? How much of an effect will it have?"

"Depends on how long they stay holed up in there."

The most important thing to do was make sure the people were blaming Cavarin for their dissatisfaction. The Allied Forces wanted the citizens to convince themselves that they were victims under Cavarin. This sentiment would grow over time and eventually pierce the container that was the city of Tholituke.

Well, it'd be pretty hard to attack the capital with a name like Liberation Front.

Their cause would appeal to people's hearts, but it made it difficult to use military force. It was a delicate situation.

"Either way, it'd be a bonus for the city. If they can put some pressure on Cavarin without getting in the way during the main event, that's enough.

Ninym entered the tent. "A report from the patrols. They've confirmed that Cavarin's forces are marching toward us."

"So they've come…"

This was the main event. Cavarin's forces were now mobilized to relieve Tholituke. Rubbing shoulders with this army had been the Allied Forces' objective.

"How many?"

"Fifteen thousand."

Zenovia trembled in her armor. But it was not because she feared an enemy army twice the size of her own.

"As you said, Prince Wein, they have under twenty thousand."

"Of course. I planned it that way." Wein smiled. "I imagine General Levert is bitterly regretting his poor situation right about now. And we're going to break his wretched heart."

——*Why did things turn out this way?*

Fifteen thousand soldiers had been sent from Cavarin to bring relief to the besieged Tholituke. However, their leader Levert had more difficulty maintaining his concentration than ever before.

The reason for this was Cavarin's current situation.

Frankly speaking, the kingdom was in danger of fracturing.

Everything, of course, began with King Ordalasse's death. The sudden loss of their leader had naturally resulted in mayhem, and the scandal that occurred right in the middle of the Gathering of the

Chosen plummeted Cavarin's international credibility. Cavarin was a feudal society. Lords and nobles grouped around the large family tree of royals, holding the nation together. However, this latest incident only exacerbated distance the lords put between themselves and the royal family of Cavarin.

This army that had been dispatched as aid was no doubt a manifestation of those circumstances. Cavarin itself could mobilize a force of over twenty thousand—and up to thirty thousand if they pushed the limits.

But Levert was here with just fifteen thousand. He had employed every possible means—and he still hadn't even been able to muster anywhere close to twenty thousand.

I have to crush these guys as soon as possible and hurry back…!

The decision to send him away from the royal capital was a sore point for Levert. The rumors that he was a king-killer trying to take over the country were still spreading among the people. This must have been the reason he was having trouble gathering lords as well. They'd try to distance themselves from Levert in the central administration and then remove the Imperial Court altogether.

However, he didn't have the choice of not going. For the aforementioned reasons, the morale of the Cavarin army was at rock bottom. Even so, they needed a general to lead them, and Levert himself would soon lose his political authority if he didn't display his skills here.

I did distance myself from King Ordalasse. But it is only because I was thinking of Cavarin.

If he wasn't here to stitch the army together at a time like this, Cavarin would become an ideal hunting ground for the other nations. If anything, he had to avoid that at all costs. That required Levert to lead their army, swiftly defeat the enemy, and return home.

I bet I'll go to hell after I die, but it's not my time yet.

He would do what he had to do. With resolve, Levert continued to march forward.

The seven thousand soldiers of the Allied Forces were arrayed against fifteen thousand men from Cavarin.

On a plain not far from Marden's former capital, the fight between the two armies started off with a surprising amount of caution. Many small-scale skirmishes unfolded as both focused on conserving their energy, and so the first day came to an end. This went on for several days. But why?

"We want to hurry up and resolve this, but Natra is famous for chasing out thirty thousand soldiers from Marden with only a small army. We'll strengthen our defenses and measure their actual skill." That would explain why Cavarin exercised caution.

"They'll try to figure us out and strengthen their defenses. Using a small number of forces to fight a battle is good for morale. We'll go along with Cavarin and fight for two or three days."

The developments so far were well within the Allied Forces' expectations.

And thus, the two sounded each other out as the third day passed. Then came the fourth day.

On this day, the battlefield would be thrown into chaos.

"Tomorrow, we take Natra down," Levert had announced to his commanders on the night of the third day during a war council.

"After a few days of fighting, I figured out their little scheme. As the rumors had it, they're powerful but not unbeatable."

The commanders nodded in agreement.

"The troops—the ones not led by the crown prince—are stiffer."

"According to our information, those are led by a general named

Raklum. It seems he was selected to replace Hagal, who was recently executed."

"Hagal was the cornerstone of Natra. His replacement might be able to control his subordinates, but there's bound to be delays. That's when we strike."

Kustavi the adjutant raised his hand. "General! In that case, I will lead the troops to take Raklum's and Wein's heads tomorrow!"

Levert's adjutant carried the blame of letting Wein get away in the past. With the accidental encounter with the rebel army, he had somehow sidestepped punishment, but it was also true that he wanted recognition of achievement more than anyone else.

However, Levert shook his head at the adjutant's eagerness.

"No, I will go myself."

"You, General?"

Kustavi wasn't the only one confused by this. The other commanders had no idea what was going on.

Levert faced them. "The homeland will grow concerned if we waste any more time. I will lead the troops to be certain everything goes as planned. Kustavi, you will trap the Remnant Army."

"If that is the case…" Kustavi nodded, looking altogether unpleased.

In actuality, half the reason behind Levert's plan was to save face. In addition to wanting to finish the battle quickly, he had a more personal reason for volunteering for the position.

"Damn Hagal… How dare he drop dead."

"General?"

"…It's nothing." Shaking his head, Levert recalled the battle-fields of his younger days.

There, he could still clearly see a free-spirited commander in his mind. He also saw himself, retreating in defeat. "Someday, I'll have your head," he remembered saying, as if to curse the enemy general.

But his foe ended up running away to a tiny northern country, and they never crossed paths again.

"…What an idiotic sentiment."

Levert stowed away this old tale that no one knew deep inside his heart.

Back at the camp for the Allied Forces, Raklum was kneeling before Wein and Zenovia.

"How are our forces, Raklum?"

Raklum replied with chagrin. "Your Highness… If you might allow me to be bold, I believe it will take them more time to accept me as Hagal's replacement…"

He had been appointed the position of general after Hagal's execution left it empty, but he regrettably could not fill his shoes. Raklum had experience leading as a captain, and he could carry out basic operations without issue. However, once he replaced Hagal, the soldiers had become wary and overly conscious of the unfamiliar relationship, and they couldn't seem to synchronize.

"I see… While it is unfortunate, I can't say it's unexpected. Don't worry about it."

"Understood…"

To Raklum, it was as if he'd failed to meet Wein's expectations. It was impossible for him not to worry—even if Wein had ordered him to a million times—but having said that, it wasn't even something he could be blamed for or improve on. And as Raklum had said, it would take time, which they didn't have.

"I'm guessing Cavarin will go all out tomorrow. That's the deadline. Tomorrow, we'll be carrying out the plan while keeping an eye on the enemy's movements. Sound good to you, Prince Helmut?"

"Of course." Zenovia gave a small nod. "Our morale is high, and we've had few casualties. If we get past their defenses, we will immobilize their main forces."

Then, with admiration, she said, "But to come up with this plan… You really are something else, Prince Wein."

"According to your younger sister, I am as much of a sham as the Holy Elites." Wein flashed her a smile. "Cavarin came at you all in one shot. Let's teach 'em a lesson."

The start of the fourth day seemed just as calm as the preceding days. However, those with sharper senses could feel the facade cracking. There was a jittery impatience disguised as calm, as if one were aiming for the enemy's throat. It was as if a piece of thread was stretched to its utmost limits, and the moment it was cut, the battlefield would become a flurry of movement.

"—All units, attack!"

Led by Levert, the five thousand soldiers pounded at the earth in their efforts to crush the troops led by Raklum.

Obviously, one side held the advantage. Not to mention that the opponent was not as fluid in their movements. The response to their charge was too slow. At this rate, they'd take the enemy general's head with one decisive stroke.

After we finish breaking through these forces, we'll swing around back and attack those led by the prince!

Levert had figured out a perfect tale for his victory. Now all that was left was to make it a reality.

But at that moment, he caught sight of one thing about the enemy before him.

Is that…?

In the center of the enemy forces was an old cavalryman. He did not have a noticeably large frame, but Levert couldn't tear his eyes away. He stood in the center of the soldiers as if he were their commander, just like on another battlefield—

In that moment, fear shivered down his spine, and Levert involuntarily shouted, "ALL UNITS, HAAAAAAALT!"

Then, General Hagal gave orders to his men.

"All units, begin."

And Natra attacked Cavarin.

"Whoa… What's happening over there?" Wein moaned as he checked on the status of the left wing.

Just as it appeared that two thousand soldiers from Natra might dodge the rush of the soldiers from Cavarin, they thrust out and entangled the enemy like a snake, taking them out one after the other. The soldiers of Cavarin had no idea what was going on.

"I knew you went easy on me, Hagal," Wein murmured in admiration.

Ninym sighed next to him. "I can't believe it… In order to launch a surprise attack against the army of Cavarin, *Hagal chose to pretend to be executed.*"

The full series of events unfolded rather curiously.

First, Ibis the merchant got in touch with the dissenters of Natra and incited a rebellion behind the scenes.

Sensing this disquieting atmosphere, Wein had implemented a plan to use Hagal and uncover the dissenters. However, it unfortunately overlapped with an invitation from Cavarin, and he had to leave the country.

Then, Ibis got in contact with Hagal, thinking he'd fit as the rebels' leader, and gathered the dissenters under him. Hagal would have been able to rout them with the fortress guards, but he would not be able to achieve more than that. He simply didn't have enough man-power to destroy them at the time.

What kind of violent activity would the rebel army think to do while Wein was away?

There was no guarantee the rebels had only gathered temporarily. In between a rock and a hard place, Hagal chose to become the leader of the rebels and take the reins.

"I will do whatever it takes as long as His Highness is able to return," he had said.

The area was heavy with rebel forces, and he was unable to contact Wein, but Hagal assumed he would come back. His first priority was Wein's return to Natra.

For that reason, Hagal formed a plan to either reduce the number of soldiers awaiting Wein on his return home or to possibly fail consolidating a chain of command. All the while, Ibis continued to get in the way.

From the battle formation of the rebel army to their erratic movements, Wein had sensed Hagal wasn't serious about betraying him. Plus, once Wein's group slipped through the rebel lines, they lured out and destroyed the rebel army with the tracks they had intentionally left behind.

It was at this time that Hagal proposed the fake death Ninym had mentioned.

Foreseeing the battle that would break out with Cavarin afterward, Hagal intentionally appeared to accept capital punishment without objection, inviting Cavarin to let their guard down. He had flipped the situation upside down.

I know it's Ibis's fault, but he's still pretty reckless.

Even if he mediated, if this plan worked out, Hagal would die a traitor and lose all his reputation and status. But Hagal—who was born in a country that prized reputation—had proposed the idea himself. This kind of resolve was not seen every day, and even Wein had no choice but to agree.

Command was then handed to Raklum until Cavarin bore down on them, and then on this fourth day, Hagal returned as general.

One could call the strategy a sweeping success. The enemy's army of five thousand was on the verge of collapse. Wein knew of Hagal's command of the flatlands, but this was truly something else.

"We better get going, Wein."

"Yeah, I'm coming."

Prompted by Ninym, Wein looked away from the left field of battle. He could now leave it up to Hagal.

"Well, I guess we better get moving, too."

The current situation was a nightmare come to life.

"General! The enemy is closing in on us!"

"Please return to the stronghold! We can't hold out here any longer!"

"Hurry! Or they'll block our escape route!"

Panicked screams layered on top of one another. But Levert knew—here there was no escape route, and everything before them was a trap laid by the enemy.

But even if he stayed, there was no future here.

"—I figured I might get taken out by a close adviser, but to think it would be the main general."

It was because the enemy general, Hagal, had already captured him.

"If you have any last words, now is your chance."

At this statement, Levert's eyes flashed. He seemed as if he might say something, but those words caught in his throat. Instead, he spoke with self-derision.

"...Even if I did, it would be a waste of breath. Now that I think about it, you got me good with that plan of yours on that day, too. I admit my loss today. —However!"

In that moment, Levert kicked his horse's sides.

"I won't die alone! You're coming to hell with me!"

Levert aimed straight for Hagal as he ran past him.

"...Sorry, but..."

As the two passed each other, Hagal's sword arm flickered like an illusion. Levert felt himself sway.

"I don't remember you at all."

Levert's body split in two, falling to the ground as blood sprayed in the air. After confirming his death, Hagal raised his sword.

"The enemy General Levert is dead!"

""YEAAAAAAAAAAH!""

The shout of victory echoed across the battlefield.

Kustavi had just pinned down the Remnant Army on the right wing and was beside himself when he heard the news.

"General Levert is dead...?!"

The only things that kept him from collapsing were his sense of responsibility to his master and his seething rage. He quickly directed his wrath toward the enemy—the Remnant Army.

"All units prepare to charge! We'll crush the Remnant Army before Natra can close in on us and regain control of this war!"

"P-please wait! Our headquarters have ordered us to retreat...!"

"Silence!" Kustavi grabbed the messenger who had tried to stop him by the collar. "Orders to ignore me and retreat?! We'll never pay them back for General Levert unless we take them down now! Tell headquarters that if they take even one step away, I'll kill everyone later!"

"B-but!"

Thrusting aside the tenacious messenger, Kustavi faced those around him and raised his voice. "Let's move! Charge!"

Five thousand soldiers obeyed Kustavi and set out. The distance between them and the Remnant Army—now on defense—narrowed in the blink of an eye, and they collided. The impact was so strong that it literally sent people flying.

"Don't stop! Push back!"

Spurred on by Kustavi, the army of Cavarin pressed forward.

Their defenses are strong, but our charge destroyed them. At this rate, we'll force them back...!

The soldiers of Cavarin slowly broke into the Remnant Army's ranks. Farther in were the enemy's main forces. Their target was the head of the enemy general, Prince Helmut. For Marden's royal family, this was a sovereign battle to take back their capital. If Cavarin took down Prince Helmut, they would lose their cause, and there was a chance his army could recover.

Just a bit more... Almost there...!

They could break through, Kustavi thought, and then he realized something.

But before he could formulate his thoughts, the enemy had wrapped around their left, right, and front.

This left only the back as an escape. As Kustavi turned around, the army of Natra was ready to charge at him, right before his eyes. They were the forces led by Wein.

"Wha——?!"

The left flank of the Cavarin army that had been crushed by Hagal resorted to using brute force to turn things around. And Wein had foreseen that.

By the time Kustavi realized he'd been lured into a trap, it was too late. Their front and sides were tightly obstructed by the Remnant Army, leaving Cavarin with nowhere to escape. They were squarely showered with a violent attack from the rear and taken out in one blow.

"D-DAMMIIIIIIIIT!"

Try as he might, Kustavi had no chance of escaping. He died in the onslaught of the soldiers of Natra, and without their commander, the remaining Cavarin soldiers lost all sense of order, driven to destruction by the two armies. As a result, the remaining soldiers defending the stronghold chose to retreat. The Allied Forces pursued them tenaciously, and it was reported that less than five thousand Cavarin soldiers escaped home to safety.

Afterward, the guards from Cavarin stationed in the Marden capital of Tholituke chose to surrender and were released. The Allied Forces were welcomed by the citizens, and this victory went down in both their nations' histories.

When Prince Wein had first visited the fortress, it was on a cold winter's day.

Someone had welcomed him warmly out of politeness, even though the figure harbored anxiety. This person was already past their prime. It wouldn't be strange at all to consider retirement, said the whispers after this banquet. Thinking about it made the commander's old bones grow cold.

Oh, why couldn't Wein have been born twenty or even ten years earlier? If he had, the soldier could have rushed around the battle-field by Wein's side—

"I bet that's what you're thinking."

The person in question jolted, agitated. Wein turned to make eye contact and spoke as if reading an open book.

"Screw age. Whether you're one or one hundred, utility is the most important. And I've never once thought of you as useless."

"……"

"Or are you already giving up on yourself? You think you can't do anything more?"

"No!" came the shout with more force than intended. Surprised by this unexpected response, the old soldier began to speak with an unbudgeable determination. "No, I would never think any such thing."

"In that case, quit worrying over nothing." Wein beamed. "Come on, Hagal. It's too soon for you to wither up and die. Let's cause trouble for this continent together."

And with that, Wein faced Hagal and held out his hand—

Light footsteps echoed like music. General Hagal was the one playing the tune. He continued without a word down the empty hallway.

The tranquil space was one of the royal villas of Natra. It was built primarily as a place for the royal family to come and rest, and it was currently occupied by only one person.

"I have come as you summoned me."

Arriving at the innermost room of the villa, Hagal bowed his head and knelt.

A large bed was before him, containing a thin man.

"...It's been a while, Hagal," the man said weakly. "I haven't seen your face in quite some time, but it looks like you're doing well."

"Yes. I was relieved to hear that Your Majesty's condition has stabilized. I pray for your swift recovery."

This was King Owen of Natra. He had been weak since birth and had most recently collapsed due to a sudden change in the weather. Even now, he recuperated in the imperial villa.

"Hagal, I called you here today for one reason alone. It concerns Wein," Owen said. "Time has passed since the country was put into his hands. How do you think he's doing?"

"Yes. Needless to say, he is gentle and firm, and his compassion has made him popular among the people. His wisdom is unfathomable to those as ordinary as me. I believe no other is more qualified than Prince Wein to rise up as the next leader of Natra."

Hagal's comments were unreserved and honest. Every word came from his heart.

"Well, then— Does he have talent worthy of your service?"

This was a complicated question, but Hagal replied without hesitation.

"Yes. If I can assist Prince Wein in his righteous rule, it would be a lifelong honor."

"I see…" There was relief in Owen's voice. "Hagal, I believe I've done you wrong. Keeping you close at hand and allowing your skills to rust away has caused me enough regret to last a lifetime."

"Not at all, Your Majesty." Hagal shook his head. "For me—a man who had wandered many years and lost my own skills—it was Your Majesty who allowed me to find a new place to belong in this land. Without you, I would have died in a nameless ditch somewhere."

Owen smiled. "I see… But you did well, Hagal. You've endured obscurity for many years. This will be my last order to you."

Owen continued. "Fly, General Hagal. Take those enormous wings and rise to the top with my son."

A flood of emotions overcame Hagal, and he bowed very, very deeply.

"Your loyal servant shall most humbly accept—"

"I see, so that's what happened. Caldmellia gave a disappointing frown as she heard the report from Ibis upon her return. "I thought we might inflict more suffering on the prince, but I understand that we cannot deal with him through ordinary means."

Kneeling before her, Ibis's expression grew grave.

"…Lady Caldmellia, I have no excuse for my failure to accomplish your task. I am prepared to accept any punishment you see fit."

At this, Caldmellia let a light smile play across her lips. "Hee-hee, punishment, huh? I have no reason at all to punish you." Caldmellia knelt and gently stroked Ibis's hair. "You are all my precious, precious children. Without you, I would simply be a mischievous old lady. Come, raise your head. Why don't we think of a plan to break this continent beyond repair? After all, enjoying life is the secret to youth."

"Yes ma'am…! Thank you, Lady Caldmellia…!"

With this, the monster bared its fangs, ready to rip apart the next story. No one yet knew where she would strike—

"AAAAND DOOOOOOOOONE!"

In an office in the royal palace of the Kingdom of Natra, Wein scraped his pen across the final sheet of paper in a pile of work, looking up at the ceiling.

"I'm finally done dealing with Cavarin, but… Agh, I seriously can't take this anymore. No more work today. I'm takin' it easy."

Wein moaned, and Ninym started to collect the documents.

"Good job. It's a good thing we were able to safely reconcile with Cavarin."

After they expelled the soldiers from Cavarin and liberated the capital of Marden, Cavarin approached the Allied Forces about the possibility of reconciliation. They'd lost the war on top of their king and begun to fall into serious instability. Deciding they could no longer fight was a smart decision on Cavarin's part.

However, the pretext for their proposed reconciliation came as a surprise. Cavarin claimed the war was all General Levert's idea and that he had been the one to kill the king. They placed all the blame on him.

On top of that, Cavarin insisted that they wished to form friendly relations with the Allied Forces. Under the conditions of reparations and mass withdrawal from former Marden territory, a peace agreement was signed.

"Couldn't you have gotten them to cough up a little more?"

"Well, that's just how things worked out. I figured other countries besides Cavarin might get involved if I got greedy." Wein sighed. There was no question the entire Western continent had been carefully observing the war. Especially leaders like the Holy Elite. He didn't want to do anything that would give them any extra excuses to intervene.

"It would have been a different story if I'd been elected as a Holy Elite, but…well, that ship has sailed."

"With this mess on the sidelines, it couldn't be helped."

Ninym was in a good mood. She had personally been against him becoming a Holy Elite, and now there was no chance in hell of it ever happening.

"That aside, I know you just completed the first load of work, but unfortunately there's still more to do."

"Ugh, what else is there?"

"A meeting with Zenovia. You can't skip out on it. See, they should already be arriving by now, so let's head to the audience hall."

Damn, that's right. Wein groaned as he got up and slouched toward the audience hall.

Once he arrived, he found Zenovia already there.

"Thanks for coming, Princess Zenovia."

Zenovia smiled as he greeted her. "I'm pleased to see you again, as well, Prince Wein."

The two continued to exchange stiff greetings. Since they were in an audience hall with the chief vassals of Natra standing nearby, this was the way things had to be.

Standing next to Wein, Ninym whispered in his ear.

"Our policies from here on should include recognition of Marden as an independent nation, right?"

"Yeah. I did promise, after all." Wein nodded and chuckled. "More than anything, with the loss of a Holy Elite throwing off the balance of power in the West, it won't be long before they crumble.

Not that I want anything to do with it. And! That's! Why! Marden will make a nice shield for our western borders."

"Wow, how unfair…"

"Nope, it's fair and square. This is what politics is all about."

As they continued their quiet exchange, Zenovia spoke up.

"…Words cannot describe our gratitude for all the assistance you provided during the war. Because of you, our ambition of taking back the royal capital has been fulfilled."

"It was nothing. I thought Cavarin was playing dirty to begin with. Besides, more than anything, it can be attributed to the zeal of the Liberation Front… It's unfortunate that Prince Helmut succumbed to his wounds from this last battle."

"Your words bring Prince Helmut peace in the next world, Your Highness."

As they had secretly agreed upon behind the scenes, Helmut was now officially deceased. Not many knew the truth.

"However, the loss of Helmut has caused unrest among the people of Marden who have only just been freed from Cavarin… I therefore have one more request."

"Ask away."

It was here that Zenovia would declare Marden's independence and her own ascension to the throne as queen, which Wein had promised to support. With this, one matter would at last be settled.

Oh, I love a happy ending. Love to work things out in a civilized manner!

A weight fell off Wein's shoulders.

"I hope you will allow our territory to swear vassalage to the Kingdom of Natra."

"…Come again?" Wein's mind froze over. Locked in place, he confirmed, "…Vassalage?"

"Yes."

Wein blinked.

The chief vassals around them stirred, and Zenovia spoke loudly enough for everyone present to hear.

"I am of the royal family of Marden, but I am only a woman and not yet capable. I do not have enough skill to lead my nation."

Through vassalage, the current Marden territory would essentially become part of Natra.

In other words, it would become a territory that Wein was duty bound to protect.

"It is clear to me that we can only survive by depending on your resourcefulness and mercy, Prince Wein. I ask that you allow us to sit at the foot of your table."

"Well, uh…"

This was a problem. A *huge* problem. His plans would all fall apart. But everything she said made it hard to turn her down. Plus, the vassals in the audience hall all nodded as if egging him on.

"Your Highness, we may have crossed swords with Marden before, but now we are brethren who fought side by side. We should accept," urged a vassal.

"Um, wai—"

"It's been two hundred years since Natra's founding… Our nation is finally making great strides."

"No, I said—"

"In this era of unrest, let's show them we're the great leaders of the north!"

"…" Wein quietly glanced at Ninym next to him.

…*Ninym, help!* he screamed silently by making intense eye contact.

There's nothing we can do. The vassals have already reached consensus, all while we've been overwhelmed with our routine duties, Ninym replied by flickering her eyes.

NYAAAAAAAGH?!

In other words, Zeno had realized Natra might use Marden as a buffer. To prevent that, she had prepared to announce the vassalage while Wein was swamped with work. Summoning Zenovia to the audience hall in Natra reinforced the fact that Natra had higher status between the two—at home and abroad. However, for her, it was the ideal opportunity to announce her intentions.

"I'm sorry. But you did say that mutual advantage was what makes a country?" Zeno whispered, sticking her tongue out subtly enough that no one else would notice.

WHY THE HELL IS THIS HAPPENING TO MEEEEEE?! Wein screamed in his heart.

Spring.

Two years after the crown prince of the Kingdom of Natra was appointed as regent.

Marden had formed an alliance with Natra and liberated its capital from Cavarin rule. And then it had declared itself a vassal of Natra.

This incident would become known as the first step toward greatness in the kingdom, and the story would be told for generations.

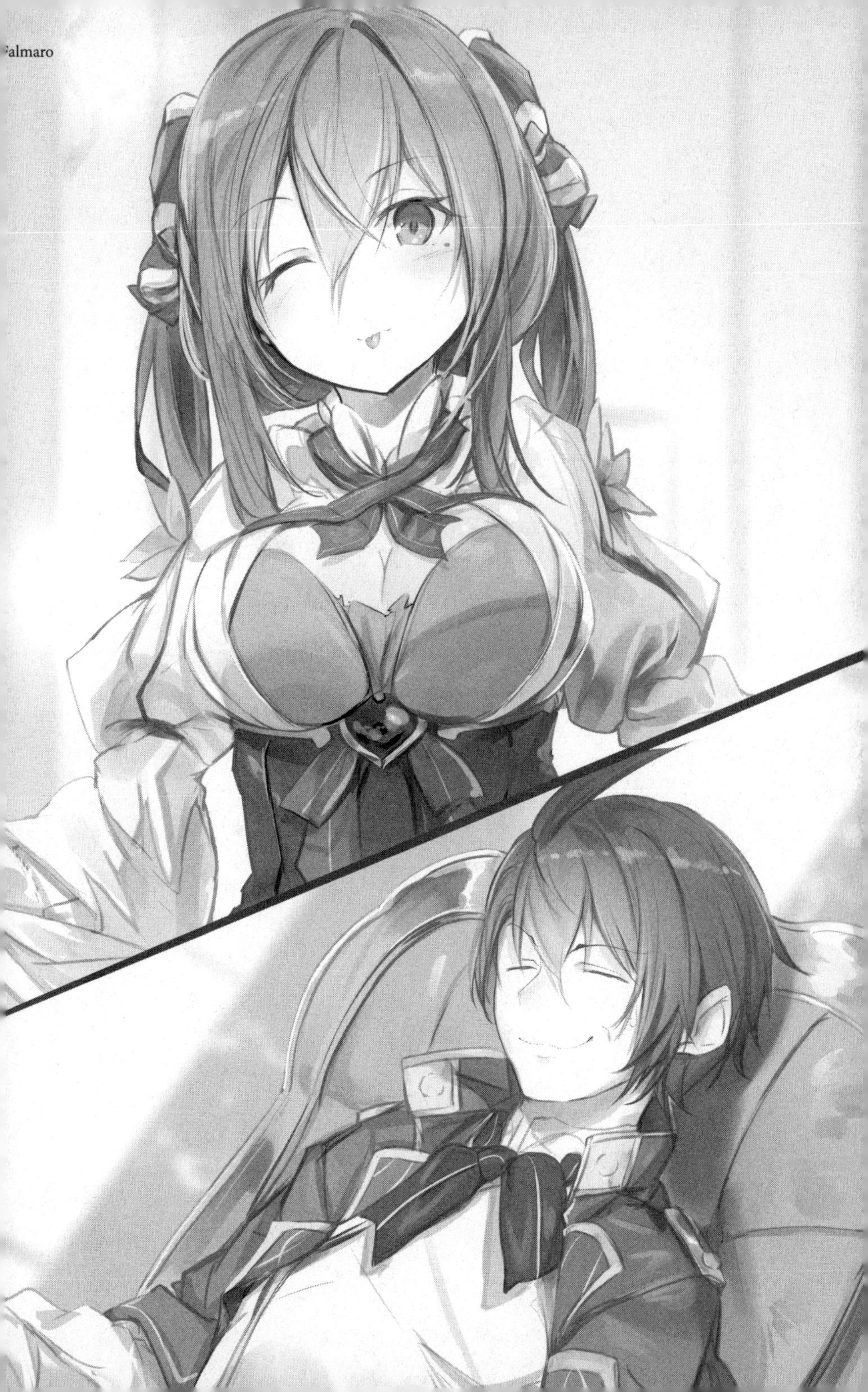

Afterword

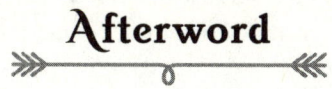

Hello, all! It has been a while. This is Toru Toba.

Thank you for picking up the third volume of *The Genius Prince's Guide to Raising a Nation Out of Debt (Hey, How About Treason?)*. Time really does fly.

In this volume, I focused on international conferences and expanding worldviews. I hope you enjoyed chance encounters with the eccentric influencers of the West and watching the series grow as a whole.

Not to digress, but I have trouble moving my hands when I'm typing. I have a bad habit of contorting my hands in unnatural angles to hit the keys. This gives me a great deal of wrist pain. To fix this, I recently bought a split keyboard. It's a keyboard that's been divided into adjustable left and right sides, which makes it possible to keep both hands perpendicular as a I feverishly type-type-type with knitted brows. This decreases wrist instability and lightens the burden on my joints. It's a great product, and it actually feels like my wrists have improved as soon as I tried it.

However, the keyboard's position was a lot different from the standard one I was used to, and I kept making typos, which was really inconvenient… I'm using it every day, so I can get used to it.

Now for the traditional thanks and apologies.

To my head editor, Ohara. I'm terribly sorry for constantly giving you trouble. The deadline was especially tight, and polishing the manuscript became a race against the clock. The third volume would not have been safely completed without your tireless efforts. Thank you very much.

I'm very grateful for my illustrator, Falmaro. Thank you again for your wonderful illustrations. When I saw the color insert, I knew they would excite the readers. More than anything, Ninym looks great with both black and white hair!

And to all the readers, thank you for your support. The third volume was able to happen because of you, and it seems there will be a next volume. It would mean so much to me if you could continue to cheer me on.

Well, it looks like next time we'll be returning to the East. Lowellmina from the second volume will be coming back, along with a lineup of all Wein's school pals… Of course, this is only tentative. It could change completely. Of course, we can cross that bridge when we come to it!

Let's meet again in the next volume.